D0189234

THE IRON CLEW

PHOEBE ATWOOD TAYLOR

WRITING AS ALICE TILTON

THE
IRON CLEW

A Leonidas Witherall Mystery

A Foul Play Press Book

THE COUNTRYMAN PRESS
Woodstock, Vermont

This edition is published in 1992 by Foul Play Press, a division
of The Countryman Press, Woodstock, Vermont 05091.

ISBN 0-88150-241-3

Printed in the United States of America on recycled paper

10   9   8   7   6   5   4   3   2   1

THE IRON CLEW

1

THE THICK BROADLOOM on the floor of his study so muffled his footsteps that Mr. Leonidas Witherall was quite unaware of making any sound at all. But in the cellar laundry room directly beneath him, his charlady Mrs. Mullet was rapidly losing her mind from listening to the broken rhythm of his restless pacing.

Eighteen steps, pause. Fourteen steps, pause.

Then eighteen more as he came down the other side of the room, another pause as he turned the corner, then fourteen steps more as he crossed by the fireplace.

That brought him back to his desk, and started him off on still another circuit.

Eighteen steps, pause, fourteen—

Mrs. Mullet gave a little cry of anguish, jerked out the electric iron plug, marched upstairs, and thrust open the study door without bothering with the formality of a knock.

"Mr. Witherall, in my candied opinion—ooh!" she broke off as he turned inquiringly toward her. "Honest, Mr. Witherall, when the light catches your face sidewise like it did just then, you're the spitting image of that new statue of Shakespeare they put into the Rivoli Theater lobby!"

"Indeed, Mrs. Mullet?" Leonidas said with absent politeness. "How kind of you to—er—drop in and divulge that fact—"

7

"Oh, I didn't come barging in to tell you about the statue! I only wanted to say that in my candied opinion, you can't expect anyone to do your ironing right when you're driving 'em crazy with all this tramping, tramping, tramping over their heads! You realize, Mr. Witherall, you been tramping around this room for two solid *hours?* What's the *matter?*"

With a gesture of weary resignation, Leonidas pointed to the fresh ream of typewriter paper on the top of his desk.

Mrs. Mullet groaned. "You're not starting another Haseltine book! Not," she added hurriedly, "that they aren't my favorite books, Mr. Witherall—but have we got to go through that again?"

"Another epic of the gallant young lieutenant," Leonidas said, "is due in the office of my new publishers in exactly four weeks."

"Four weeks?" Mrs. Mullet brightened. "Oh, then you don't need to start *now!* You got anyway ten days before you have to break down and begin—why, they haven't even pestered you with letters and telegrams about it yet, have they?"

"That," Leonidas took off his pince-nez and began to twirl them slowly on the end of their broad black ribbon, "is the problem. They haven't badgered me at all. They merely assume that the manuscript will be done on time. Curiously enough, I find myself hesitant to destroy such delightful naïveté. It's my intention to start that book at once. Only," he smiled ruefully, "I can't start!"

"You always say that, every book," Mrs. Mullet reminded him. "But you always *do* start. This time isn't any different."

"Ah, but it is!" Leonidas said. "Consider, Mrs. Mullet, how thwarting this brave new world is to a character like the fiery Lieutenant Haseltine. Take the—er—achievement of Atomic Power, on which I've relied so often for plots in the past—you know," he went on explanatorily, "some sinister foreign government would be about to loose some infernal atomic machine on the world, and Haseltine, with the aid of the beauteous Lady Alicia and Faithful Frank, somehow ferreted out the diabolic details, grabbed The Thing in the nick of time, and saved humanity for yet another volume. But now that The Thing actually exists, I can't use it!"

"There's always Japs," Mrs. Mullet suggested. "Think what lovely times Haseltine had foiling Admiral Yamaguchi!"

"M'yes. I fear, however," Leonidas said, "that the fiendish Nipponese are slightly on the moth-eaten side at this point. Vindictive armament kings like our useful old friend Count Casimir, world-hungry dictators like our malevolent Dolphin—all are passé, Mrs. Mullet. Old hat, in a nutshell."

"How about South American revolutions?" she asked hopefully. "Or Red plots?"

Leonidas shook his head. "We're Good Neighbors," he said with a sigh, "and this is One World. No, I've tramped this room for miles, brooding vigorously every inch of the way, and I can conjure up nothing from which Haseltine can rescue Lady Alicia and humanity. Absolutely nothing. In one hundred and seven volumes, the gallant lieutenant has never before been forced to cope with the simple toys of peace."

"Well," Mrs. Mullet said, "well, I see what you mean.

But if you got to cope with peace, you might as well make the best of it. Why *not* mix Haseltine up with simple things for a change? You know, like murder, and robbery. Be a nice change from world intrigue, like. And instead of Atom Bombs, just mysterious *little* things."

"Er—could you," Leonidas inquired, "name three?"

"Brown paper packages," Mrs. Mullet said at once. "*Mysterious* brown paper packages. Three of 'em."

"Brown paper packages?" Leonidas put on his pince-nez and stared at her. "Oh, come now, Mrs. Mullet! After all the blood and thunder of Haseltine's past, what reader would care two figs for even *one* mysterious brown paper package, let alone three?"

"*I* would."

"After Atom Bombs and stolen treaties, and emeralds worth a king's ransom bandied about like so much buttered pop corn, you actually can find something intriguing in a mysterious brown paper package?"

"That's right, Mr. Witherall. I never see a brown paper package I don't start going crazy wondering what's in it. After those vipers, you know," she added casually.

"Vipers?" Leonidas tried to match her nonchalance. "Er—did you say *vipers*, Mrs. Mullet?"

She nodded. "You know. Snakes, like. There was this nice old white-haired lady sat next me on a Pomfret bus one day, about eight years ago," she went on reminiscently. "Had this brown paper package on her lap. It looked just like two pounds of Fanny Farmer's to me, but then something started scratching and wriggling, and out come this viper. Then nine more."

Leonidas leaned back in his desk chair.

"Upon occasion," he remarked, "I find myself wondering if you are possibly not more qualified to create Haseltine than I. Why, Mrs. Mullet? Why ten vipers?"

"She raised 'em for a living," Mrs. Mullet said simply. "Sold 'em to laboratories—that's where she was carrying the things, to some research place. She said it was nice easy work and paid good. No, Mr. Witherall, I don't know as there's anything tantalizes me more than a mysterious brown paper package. Like the one that came this noon." She pointed to a small, flat, unopened brown paper-wrapped package on the table by the study door.

Leonidas smiled. "Much as I hate to disillusion you," he said, "that contains one of Fenwick Balderston's lengthy dissertations on the investments of the Dalton Safe Deposit and Trust Company. As a director, I receive one every quarter, and I can assure you that a small nest of vipers would be considerably livelier and unquestionably more amusing."

"But you haven't opened it!" she protested. "You don't *know* it's that bank thing—and it didn't come by the bank messenger, like it usually does, either. It was brought by a beautiful young *girl!*"

"Indeed?"

"A blonde, too." Mrs. Mullet ignored his irony. "Just like the Lady Alicia. Only she had grey eyes instead of blue, and she wore harlequin glasses with thick green rims, and a green suit with round silver buttons. She came in one of those fancy beachwagon convertibles —don't you want me to open it for you?"

"Emphatically not," Leonidas said. "Because if you did, my conscience would force me to read the thing in its dull entirety, whereas if I leave it until ten minutes before I set out for my dinner date with Balderston tonight, I can with impunity merely initial the pages. No, Mrs. Mullet, even if that package had arrived on a golden platter perched on the trunk of a rajah's elephant, I should still know it was only that idiot report. Er—didn't you observe the bank's label?"

"There was a label on those vipers," Mrs. Mullet returned. "It said, 'Dainty Confections from Aunt Dora's Homestyle Cupboard.' The woman told me she'd had it around her desk a long time, and it was all she could find to stick up the end of the package with. Maybe this bank label just *happ*ened—"

"No," Leonidas said. "Er—no! The Dalton Bank, which suspiciously chains its pens to its writing desks, would never, never permit a label to escape into the clutches of any unauthorized person. Besides, Balderston phoned me to expect that report. Getting back to the simple issues of murder and robbery, have you read any good murders lately, Mrs. Mullet?"

"No good ones. They're all—well, to coin a phase, they're all so awful *gutty,* Mr. Witherall! So—so—what would be the right word?"

"Uninhibited, perhaps?"

"I guess that's it. Honest, I can't remember when a detective hasn't knocked the heroine onto a couch before he even knows her last name! My niece that's staying with me now, she's given up murders. She just went back to *Sexy Tales* and *Passionate Love Weekly*—nice stories like those. You know."

"M'yes," Leonidas said. "The wholesome school. Do I gather that you wouldn't care to have Haseltine appear in an uninhibited or gutty production?"

Mrs. Mullet shook her head vigorously. "I should say not! In my candied opinion, Lady Alicia wouldn't stand for no adolitry—not her! Besides, Mr. Witherall, when all's said and done, there's only one way to commit adolitry. But murder, now, *that's* got some variety to it! Start Haseltine off with a nice quiet murder that begins with something simple, like a mysterious brown paper pack— oh, I forgot!" she broke off as the mantel clock struck four, "do you mind if I go early this afternoon? I got a kind of an interesting job I'm taking over for a friend of mine tonight—"

She paused, obviously wanting him to ask for further details, but Leonidas merely nodded as he eyed the ream of typewriter paper.

"Certainly, Mrs. Mullet. Leave whenever you wish. And don't forget that we have to entertain the Collectors' Club tomorrow evening—you've ordered the sandwiches and found someone to assist you, I trust?"

"My niece's coming, and everything's all ordered and all set—honest, Mr. Witherall, you're not going to fret any more about Haseltine today, are you?"

Leonidas assured her with sincerity that he harbored no such intention.

But after she left the room, he found himself fixedly and thoughtfully contemplating Balderston's brown paper package.

After a few minutes, he pivoted his desk chair around to the typewriter table.

Mrs. Mullet, about to leave by the kitchen door, winced at the sound of the machine's keys clicking merrily away

"That man!" she muttered. "That *man!*"

Once he got going like that, he'd never in the world remember his dinner date. Probably he wouldn't even remember dinner at all.

Acting on sudden impulse, she reached up and unplugged the electric kitchen clock, and set its alarm for six-thirty. Then, tiptoeing into the hall, she plugged the clock into an outlet just beyond the study door.

"There!" she said to herself with satisfaction as she left the house. "That'll at least keep on ringing and bothering him until he gets up and stops it, and once he's up, he ought to stay up!"

When the alarm went off, the study bore only a cursory resemblance to the tidy, well-ordered room of a few hours before. The broadloom floor covering had all but disappeared under a litter of books—textbooks, almanacs, magazines, copies of the Encyclopaedia Britannica. Five old Haseltine volumes stood propped open on the mantel, and life-size illustrations of the gallant lieutenant and his beauteous Alicia hung over a chair back. The wastebasket, itself quite empty, was now an island surrounded by a sea of crumpled, discarded sheets of typing paper. The air was thick with a blue haze of pipe smoke.

Leonidas, consulting a map spread over the window seat, merely frowned at the clamorous pealing. Finally, when it gave no indication of abating during his lifetime, he looked up and started to summon Mrs. Mullet.

Then, remembering her early departure, he strode out into the hall, where he promptly stubbed his toe on the still-ringing clock.

"Now why," he murmured as he picked it up and turned off the alarm, "why should the excellent Mullet have set this thing—oh!" He noted the time. "Of course,

14

she didn't wish me to forget my engagement with Balderston! How very considerate of her. M'yes, indeed!"

He hummed lightly under his breath as he went upstairs to wash and to change his clothes. No matter how he dreaded the actual labor and the mental wear and tear of a full-length book manuscript, he always found the preliminary process of sorting things out both pleasurable and stimulating. This new Haseltine, revolving around three brown paper packages and involving three different sets of people, was—in this embryonic stage, at least—a veritable little technical gem.

Rather, he thought as he turned on the shower, a pea-and-shell game with brown paper packages.

There'd be a corpse, of course. A prominent corpse, possibly a senator. At all events a man of property and substance and repute. A Man of Distinction, whose brutal murder would cause Lowell Thomas and Gabriel Heatter to rub their hands in glee. On purely esthetic grounds, he had dismissed the alternate possibility of having his victim a Woman of Importance. Women of Importance were so inclined to resemble Wagnerian sopranos that a description of their large, inert forms tended toward comic-opera.

And how would Haseltine himself fit in?

"On leave, recuperating from his wounds," Leonidas critically surveyed his beard in the bathroom mirror. "Circumstantially implicated, falsely accused, backed by fate into a corner from which there is no escape, the gallant officer turns detective. Beset by pitfalls, relentlessly pursued—"

Perhaps, to keep pace with the times, he should throw in one slightly gutty girl character. Someone named

Gypsy, or Scarlett, or Brenda, or Lauren. The trick would be to write her so inoffensively that any reader who wanted to stay awake and pant could do so, and the rest could sleep as soundly as they wished.

His mood of slight elation began to wane as he considered the prospect of dining with Fenwick Balderston in that morgue of a house with its stained-glass windows and mahogany panelling and black marble mantels. Not that he had anything against Balderston. The man was a pillar of Dalton, a pillar of the state. Dalton had originally been called Balderstown, and the hill section near the Country Club was still called Balderstown Acres, after the estate of one of Fenwick's pre-Revolutionary ancestors. Anyone who said a harsh word against any Balderston in the city of Dalton would be clapped without further ado into the psychopathic ward of the Balderston Memorial Hospital on Balderston Avenue. That Mrs. Mullet had laid out his dinner jacket was some indication of the average individual's reaction toward dining at Balderston Hall.

Why, Leonidas asked himself curiously, should he invariably have this negative feeling toward Fenwick? The man wasn't dull. He wasn't—wasn't—

He paused in the act of extracting a shoe tree and tried to summon up some proper adjectives.

"How appalling!" he said at last. "I can't honestly think of anything else to say about him! Is it possible that I attend these quarterly dinners because Fenwick possesses an incomparable cook?"

It was the truth, and he had always known it was the truth, had merely never permitted himself to let the truth slip out into the light of day. There was absolutely nothing derogatory to be said about Fenwick as a man, a bank president, or as a personage. Conversely, when one attempted a positive, straight-from-the-heart statement about Fenwick, his cook was the only factor to inspire enthusiasm.

Leonidas consoled himself by reflecting that he had worked hard at being a director of Fenwick's bank, that he actually had earned those dinners, and that this was, after all, the last quarter of his last term. A few short months would see the end of this, the last of the wartime jobs which had been foisted on him during the depths of the man-power shortage. He was already free of the Bide-a-Wee Cat and Dog Home Supervisorship, the Greens Committee Chairmanship, the Dalton Board for Better Movies, and all the rest.

Once this new Haseltine manuscript and Fenwick's directorship were wiped off the boards, he could devote himself wholeheartedly to the general welfare and the physical expansion of Meredith's Academy, the boys' school which he had inherited from his old friend Marcus Meredith. A new dormitory and a new science building headed his agenda, but his first Herculean task would be that of wangling the gift of fifty acres from the new owner of Fairlawns, the adjoining property. Mrs. Goldthwaite had not yet arrived in Dalton to take up residence, but if she proved to be one-half the advertised combination of miser, shrew and termagant, his preliminary plans for extracting those acres would have to exceed in ingenuity any Haseltine plot he had ever thus far devised.

After a brief but successful tussle with his tie, Leonidas came downstairs, donned his chesterfield, and set his best black Homburg at a jaunty angle. From the rack of canes by the front hall closet, he chose a silver-knobbed Malacca stick as being eminently suited to his role of bank director and Balderston dinner guest.

At the front door, he stopped and snapped his fingers. "The package!" he said. "That infernal report!"

Turning on his heel, he entered the cluttered study and reached out his hand toward the table by the door.

His poised hand froze in mid-air.

The brown paper package was gone.

2

LEONIDAS CLOSED HIS EYES, slowly counted to twenty, and looked again at the table top.

Then he looked under the table, and behind it.

No package.

Even a careful polishing of his pince-nez with a fresh linen handkerchief in no way altered what he saw—or rather, he mentally amended, what he didn't see— through them.

The brown paper package was gone.

"Gone, period," he said.

Setting his cane and his Homburg down on a leather-covered armchair, Leonidas perched on the arm and told himself firmly that this was really a very simple problem whose solution only depended on his ability to recall the most elementary of details.

Where had the brown paper package been when he last saw it?

Right on that table, the answer came rolling back at him, right on that table!

Leonidas removed his chesterfield.

"Let us," he murmured, "let us reconstruct. The package was most assuredly on that table when Mrs. Mullet left."

Was it?

In her zeal for learning the contents of brown paper-wrapped packages, could she possibly— Leonidas shook his head. In the eight years during which she had washed, ironed, cleaned, cooked and dusted for him, he had never once found any occasion to question her integrity. Her marketing and household accounts were always balanced, she practically never removed an egg from the refrigerator without apprising him of the act, she had never even breathed a word to anyone about his being Morgatroyd Jones, creator of the dauntless Haseltine. To assume for a moment that she had anything whatever to do with the removal of this package was idiotic!

"The package was there when she left. The package was there when I went upstairs. The package is not there now."

An expression of deep preoccupation settled over his face as he walked to his desk and shuffled around among the litter of papers.

"M'yes." He picked up a sheet headed "Chap. 1, Disa & Data," and read the notations aloud in a pensive voice. " 'Package in room first, package in room when X leaves, package gone when X returns.' M'yes, indeed. It seemed to me that I'd written this somewhere before!"

Continued reflection over such a coincidence, he thought grimly, could only lead to straitjackets, padded cells, and doubtless the shock treatment also.

This report of Balderston's couldn't be "gone"! It was misplaced. Probably, in some absent-minded moment while he was checking through old Haseltines for background information, he himself must have moved the report elsewhere. Not that he had the slightest recollection of doing anything of the sort, but he must have.

As he let the page of his first chapter's tentative plans

flutter down on the desk top, another sheet, typed in upper case capitals, seemed to float up from the clutter and hit him in the eye.

"DEVICES?" it asked insinuatingly. "CLOCK? WHY NOT TIME ENTRY OF INTRUDER WHO FIRST STEALS PACKAGE BY JERKED-OUT ELECTRIC CLOCK? CLOCK CORD SHOULD *NOT* TRIP THIEF (MUST NOT CAUSE NOISE & SPOIL INITIAL SUR-PRISE OF PACKAGE'S DISAPPEARANCE) BUT UN-WITTING INTRUDER SOMEHOW LEAVES REC-ORD OF PRESENCE & TIMING OF SAME BY PULLED-OUT CLOCK CORD. HOW TO SITUATE THIS CLOCK CONVENIENTLY TO ACHIEVE SUCH A RESULT? *THINK!!*"

A split second later, Leonidas was out in the hall, staring at the clock which Mrs. Mullet had so consider-ately left on the floor, the clock whose alarm he had turned off before he went upstairs.

Its cord had been jerked out of its baseboard outlet.

And the hands had thereby been stopped at exactly ten minutes to seven.

In short, while he was upstairs dressing, a short fifteen minutes ago, someone actually had entered his house and stolen the brown paper package!

Leonidas leaned back against the wall and started to laugh softly.

"The old octopus of fate!" he said. "M'yes, unquestion-ably!"

That old octopus of fate, a description of whose viscous tentacles often took up half a page in Haseltine when he was hard pressed to pad out a chapter, had obviously slithered out from his printed words and into his own

21

personal and private life. Dyed-in-the-wool Haseltine fans hailed the creature's appearance in much the same fashion in which Columbus's lookout greeted the sight of the New World. It marked the dividing line where the blurred edges of reality began to cross over and join the indistinct boundaries of fiction. From the old octopus onward, anything could happen—and usually did, with no holds barred.

Certainly, Leonidas thought, the edges of this particular reality could reasonably be described as beginning to blur when some idiot intruder entered his house apparently for the sole purpose of making away with Fenwick Balderston's completely unimportant report! Considering that the investment policies of the Dalton Bank hadn't changed appreciably in a hundred years, considering that one report was a virtual twin of its predecessor, that any curious passerby might read the latter merely by entering the bank and marching over to the copy hanging by the Receiving Teller's window, this theft was neither very realistic in its purpose nor very dramatic in a fictional sense.

"And how did our package-snatcher gain entrance, I wonder?" He glanced toward the front door, which clearly had not been tampered with. "By the back door, I dare say. M'yes—"

He was snapping on the kitchen light to investigate when he heard the quick, sharp slam of a closing door.

A *door?*

Leonidas paused.

What door?

It had sounded like—yes, it *was* his own front door!

22

His pince-nez, apparently sharing his astonishment, bounced from his nose.

So the intruder hadn't at once departed after snatching that package? So he had been lurking somewhere in the house all this time, and was only just now achieving his getaway?

Leonidas raced back through the hall, flung open the front door, and rushed headlong down the flagstone path to the sidewalk.

To either side of him, Birch Hill Road was still and quiet and deserted under the pale November moon.

No scurrying figure scrunched along the gravel sidewalk, no one slunk around the yellow puddles of light under the street lamps, no urgent sound of fleeing footsteps punctuated the silence. There wasn't even a sinister scuffle of dried leaves, or a crackling of little twigs.

To all intents and purposes, whoever had exited by his front door had promptly melted into the cool autumn air.

Leonidas nodded appreciatively.

Faced with similar circumstances, he would have attempted to create just such an impression, himself. It was an old Haseltine custom to deliver sage clichés on the inadvisability of beating clumsy or hasty or obvious retreats.

"When you run," the gallant lieutenant often said chidingly to Faithful Frank, "you are wrong. Dogs, policemen and small boys automatically give chase, and shrill cries of 'Stop thief!' resound about your ears. Public opinion is against you. So never abandon yourself to blind flight. Climb above trouble. Wait for it to pass."

Leonidas looked up and thoughtfully surveyed the surrounding trees.

But neither the thin white birches nor the gaunt oaks with a few tenacious leaves still flapping on their stubby, hurricane-scarred branches offered any practical sort of refuge to anyone desirous of sitting out a tense interlude.

His high barberry hedge was good but too prickly, and his lilac clumps were far too spindly for adequate concealment.

But the evergreen planting near the house, always thick with shadows, might very easily be harboring his late visitor.

And probably was, Leonidas decided without turning his head to stare in that direction.

Should he make some attempt to root the fellow out?

He projected a mental moving picture of himself engaging in the quick turn, the sudden dart—and the fruitless pounce. While he industriously searched one yew after another yew, the package-snatcher, containing his mirth with difficulty, deftly moved from one hemlock to another hemlock. While he pounced on the hemlocks and combed them in turn, the package-snatcher sidestepped and slid into the yews. That was the sort of absurd, Musical Chairs problem which always ensued when one's quarry had the tactical advantage of being able to view every move made by his pursuer.

Should he then summon the police, like a proper Dalton citizen?

The Birch Hill prowl car would undoubtedly arrive with its usual celerity and screeching of brakes. Leonidas freely conceded Sergeant MacCobble his reputation of always being the first on the scene of any given crime. But while MacCobble was roaring out to his rookie companion loud and explicit instructions on the technique of surrounding a rhododendron thicket, the intruder would be sensibly utilizing the noise and confusion to cover up his own movements, in wending his way to a more relaxing atmosphere. By the time the sergeant had finished shouting and stamping around, the object of his search would probably have reached the neighboring town of Pomfret, en route to Framfield and far points west.

Having thus dismissed as impracticable both the direct individual pounce and the conventional group or police approach, Leonidas put on his pince-nez, squared his shoulders, and set to work achieving a typical Haseltine solution to his little problem.

Turning to his right, he marched briskly along Birch Hill Road, past the Bolsters' white colonial, past the Washburns' yellow colonial, past the Pushings' large, dung-colored stucco edifice on the corner.

Once around the corner, he stopped abruptly in the lush shadow of the Pushings' overhanging red tile roof, and listened. Then he tiptoed back to the corner as far as the Pushings' mountain ash tree, and peeked toward his own house.

The figure of a woman appeared suddenly in the vicinity of his front door—rather, Leonidas thought, as if she'd sprung up through the lawn from some subterranean Jack Horner pie—and started hurrying down his flagstone path.

"She *was* hiding in the yews!" he murmured with satisfaction. "Now—left, or right? If she turns to the left, I feel sure it will be because she watched me turn this way!"

He was far too busily absorbed to notice the astonished face of Yeoville Pushing staring at him from the casement windows of the Pushings' living room.

This woman was not young, Leonidas observed, she was on the stoutish side, she had the slightly stiff-legged gait that seemed to accompany exorbitantly high heels, and there was no reason for him to assume that catching up with her would present any difficulties whatsoever.

"Left! M'yes, I thought so!"

Leonidas smiled and started around the corner just as Yeoville Pushing called to his wife to come quick and see what in the world she thought that Witherall fellow was up to now.

In retracing his steps along Birch Hill Road, Leonidas kept carefully on the turf edge of the gravel sidewalk. Moving quietly, and with no more effort than lengthening his normal stride, he was within six feet of overtaking the woman before she reached the Bracketts' grey colonial, two houses beyond his own.

Closer scrutiny was confirming his first impression that she was both middle-aged and a good size forty. That dimensional guess was on the charitable side, too, for her girth was most unkindly accentuated by a bulky mink coat. Her hat, a tall silly thing shaped like a chopped-off stovepipe, had tricked him into thinking that she was quite tall. Actually, she couldn't be an inch over five feet.

He continued silently along behind her, listening to her unbelievably high heels as they dug into the gravel, and feeling almost hypnotized by the swaying, parsley-like decorations on her hat, which nodded back at him amiably at every step.

Slung over her left shoulder was a mammoth alligator bag, roughly three times the size of an ordinary knapsack, which kept bobbing wildly off her hip as if it were trying to escape her by jumping away.

His purloined brown paper package, Leonidas decided, would be lurking somewhere in the cavernous depths of that expensive portmanteau.

An awkward possibility suddenly occurred to him and caused him to frown thoughtfully.

Suppose that when he accosted her, as he intended to when they reached the comparative privacy of the vacant lot by the next corner, suppose that she chose to brazen the situation out? Suppose she refused to accede to his peremptory demand to hand over his package, denied any knowledge of it, and threatened to call the police?

Leonidas bit his lip.

While his Haseltinian devices for forcing the hiding package-snatcher out in the open had unquestionably brought forth excellent results, he was forced to admit to himself that this elegantly dressed individual, whose Chanel Number Five was beginning to asphyxiate him, was not precisely his preconceived picture of a common sneak thief. He should hardly expect her, when stopped and challenged, to act like one.

With reluctance, he decided that he ought to have allowed for some variation in type, and that he ought to have run after her howling with indignation, letting the neighborhood think what it might.

In brief, perhaps he had been just a shade too clever!

He was barely able to stifle the exclamation which leapt to his lips when he suddenly realized, as the woman hitched something up under the arm of her right coat sleeve, that the brown paper package was right there, right out in the open, right under his nose!

He wasn't going to be forced into any melodramatic dialogue, or into making any forceful demands about her opening that pocketbook, after all.

A situation fraught with potential complexities had resolved itself into one of exquisite simplicity.

Darting forward, Leonidas made a deft, firm grab at the package.

It was his own package, he found as he held it up to the streetlight, bearing the Dalton Bank's distinctive bordered label.

"I'm so sorry," he said with ironic courtesy as the woman swung around and faced him, "so very sorry to startle you, but I actively resent being looted of even so unimport—"

A piercing whistle blasted out over Birch Hill Road.

It was the woman, tootling furiously on a diminutive whistle which materialized so quickly that Leonidas could only guess that it must have been dangling from a chain around her neck.

"So unimportant a package," Leonidas continued, raising his voice above the blasts, "as this one. You are obviously laboring under a misap—"

He broke off as an extremely long, extremely low black sedan, a shining vehicle out of an advertising man's dream world, whirled around the corner and came to a stop beside them.

Two men—two extremely large men—jumped out.

Leonidas had a jumbled impression of uniforms, visored caps, and brass buttons.

"This man has stolen my package," the woman informed them simply, in conversational tones. "Get it."

"Madam," Leonidas began, "you—"

"Get it!" the woman repeated.

With the two men advancing on him in a menacing fashion, Leonidas took a step backward.

Then another.

And another.

Suddenly, against every precept in the Haseltine code of stalwart action, he found himself running pell-mell down Birch Hill Road, with the two men pounding after him in violent pursuit.

Before he reached the Bracketts' grey colonial, he had been grabbed at twice, but each time he managed to duck and get away.

But in front of the Emersons' English brick, Leonidas knew he was lost.

Then John L. Lewis, against whom Leonidas had so often fumed, took it into his capricious head to join in the fun.

John L., the Emersons' boxer, was a dog who lived to romp. If fellow-rompers weren't at hand, he created his own diversional activities, which ranged widely throughout the animal, vegetable and mineral kingdoms. Your shoe, your garden, your roast, or you, in person—John L. had as much happy satisfaction tearing one apart as another.

Apparently sensing kinship with these two large vigorous newcomers, John L. ignored Leonidas as an old, routine occupant of his bailiwick, and devoted himself to a prideful display of his energy and strength for the benefit of his brothers.

His obstreperous delaying action was sufficiently successful to enable Leonidas to round Pushing's corner well in advance of the pair.

From the rising clamor, however, he knew that the simple posse of two was already developing into a sizable man-hunt. Other dogs were now trying to out-yelp John L., new voices were resounding, the crunch of sidewalk gravel was growing to the proportions of static. Cries of "Stop thief!" gave way to demands for "Police!"

Panting along with the brown paper package gripped to him, Leonidas decided that his only possible chance of eluding his pursuers lay in confusing them. If he could reverse his field and double back through the back yards, he might perhaps achieve the comparative haven of his own garage, from which he could whip unseen into the house, don his hat and coat, and maybe—maybe he might even sally forth to join the hunt as an innocent bystander. That would certainly be the easiest way to prove his entire lack of complicity in this affair!

But as he swerved blindly into the nearest driveway on Great Oak Road, he realized the remoteness of any such flamboyant, Haseltinian finale.

He was winded.

Utterly, completely, devastatingly winded.

He couldn't maintain this furious pace another two steps.

His lungs were bursting. He couldn't see. Bass drums were booming in his ears.

A coupé parked just outside the garage ahead loomed indistinctly before his eyes.

Gasping and choking, he managed to open the door, somehow stumbled inside, and huddled down on the floor.

3

W ITH HIS FIRST FULL BREATH, Leonidas began to regret his hasty action. With his second, he began to berate himself soundly.

He never should have backed away from that pair in the first place. He should have stood his ground. This was *his* package. *He* was right!

And never, never should he have permitted a momentary breathlessness to land him in a position as idiotic as the one in which he now found himself. Never!

His cheeks and ears began to burn at the thought of what a clambake, fish fry and general field day his discovery would provide for the neighbors. While he had no doubt of his inherent rightness and of his ultimate exoneration by the police and everyone else, the intervening interlude was going to prove very, very trying to his dignity. The Meredith's Academy boys in particular would appreciate—and never forget, or let him forget—the *Dalton Chronicle's* account of his being found in a disheveled condition, huddling on the floor of a strange coupé, clasping a Dalton bank report to his bosom.

The driveway now sounded as if it were crawling with hordes of people, and dogs, yelping practically at his heels, added a reminiscent aura of "Uncle Tom's Cabin" to the noise and confusion.

Then someone grabbed the door handle.

At the click of the latch, Leonidas sighed and braced himself for the forthcoming ordeal.

"A man? Running?" The voice, which sounded so near, obviously must belong to the man whose hand was on the door handle. "Yes, I know where he is. I'll show you. Come here."

At this point in a Haseltine epic, Leonidas thought with some bitterness, the old octopus of fate would beneficently intervene and miraculously rescue the gallant lieutenant. That was the advantage of malleable fiction over unrelenting fact!

"Look—see that tennis court across the street, there? He cut through that." As the man continued, Leonidas felt his jaw sag in amazement. "Over to Maple Street—what? Why didn't *I* stop him for you? I couldn't! I only saw him from an upstairs window!"

The car door opened, an overcoat was flung down on top of Leonidas, and a man got in and started the motor just in time to drown out the hearty and involuntary exclamation of relief that issued from the floor.

"You people mind moving so I can back?" the man called out. "And will someone grab that dog? Thanks."

The coupé backed down the driveway, swung around.

When it finally came to a stop, Leonidas guessed that a good mile had been inserted between it and the Birch Hill district.

"Now, Bill Shakespeare, I think it's safe for you to come out!" The man had started off merely sounding amused, but he ended by breaking out into a roar of laughter. "Oh, God, *how* I used to dream of something like this happening when I was in the Fifth Form!"

"May I say," Leonidas unwound himself from the overcoat and raised himself up onto the car seat, the while still gripping his brown paper package, "that I am deeply, deeply grateful for your most generous and thoughtful assistance?" He fumbled for his pince-nez, put them on, and looked interestedly at the coupé's driver. To the best of his recollection, he had never seen this pug-nosed young man before in his life. "Er—do I gather that you are a Meredith Old Boy?"

"I'm an *ex*-Meredith Old Boy. You asked dad to remove me in the Fourth. But what I learned, I learned hard. 'Brothers all, united stand,'" he sang out with gusto in a pleasant tenor, "'always give a forward hand, for the honor, for the glory of the schoooool! Fling the azure banner high, Meredith spirit shall ne'er die—'" he broke off. "Whom did you murder, Mr. Withcrall? And please *do* note that 'whom'!"

"I didn't," Leonidas returned.

"Oh. Simple assault and battery, maybe? Or was it just mayhem they were after you for?"

"The nubbin of all that confusion was this small brown paper package of mine." Leonidas displayed it. "Er—regretfully, in the process of retrieving it from an unknown woman, complications arose. Mm—sacked in the Fourth Form, you say? Are you Harriman, with the predilection for assembling Fords on the bottom of the empty swimming pool, and leaving them there?"

"You're warm. That was my cousin Bill, or the brilliant, slightly anti-social Harriman. I'm John, the dumb, or football branch of the family. I flunked every subject every semester, but I got the Founder's Medal for Pleasant Personality and Unremitting Diligence—look, sir, what's *in* that silly little package, a million dollars or something?"

33

"An unimportant report of the investments of the Dalton Safe Deposit and Trust Company," Leonidas said. "For reasons not clear to me, it was filched from my study by an intruder—" He paused as the carillon of St. Julia's, in the next block, played its half-hour tune. "Is it nine-thirty, or ten-thirty?"

"Why," Harriman said, "it's only *seven*-thirty! Oh, yes, sir, I'm quite sure. I know. It was only seven-twentyish when we withdrew from the scene of your action. Look, I don't understand how—"

"Seven-thirty!" Leonidas said wonderingly. "Is it possible that all that to-do occurred in a mere quarter of an hour? I suppose it only *seems* as though I'd spent the better part of my life huddled on the floor of this car! Harriman, are you en route to some urgent business?"

"Just an errand for my aunt. Nothing at all vital. Why?"

"I'd quite lost sight of the fact that I had a dinner engagement—indeed, without St. Julia's chimes and your reassurance as to the time, I would have assumed that I'd missed the date entirely. Could you possibly drive me over to Fenwick Balderston's?"

"Sure. Glad to. Where is it?"

"Over by the Country Club, on Kenilworth Road. With your cooperation, I shall arrive mussed and untidy, but only a few minutes late. On the whole—m'yes," Leonidas said, "I think it might be unwise of me to return home to spruce up and get my hat and coat."

"If you'll just guide me beyond the club—honestly, Bill Shakespeare, I couldn't believe my eyes when I looked out the window and saw you, of all people, staggering into the drive! I've never forgotten that beard of yours.

34

Matter of fact," he added as he started the car, "I might as well confess that it's practically my only contact with Shakespeare. Look, I can't get this straight! If someone stole that package *from* you, how come it's *you* being pursued by half of Dalton Centre and all of its dogs?"

Leonidas gave him a succinct résumé of the brown paper package's history, its disappearance, its reappearance under the arm of the be-minked lady with the stovepipe hat, of the car that magically rolled up in response to her whistling, of the two men who went for him, and of the noble part played by the romping John L. Lewis during his pell-mell rush to elude them.

"The rest," he concluded, "you—er—know."

"You're really making it up as you go along, aren't you, sir?" Harriman asked politely. "I mean, *why* should anyone creep into your house for a bank report that you claim isn't worth a hoot? Particularly a character like this plushy mink job—what in God's name would she *want* with it?"

Leonidas shrugged. "I can't imagine! We can only charitably assume that it was all an elaboration of the mistaken identity situation. Perhaps she meant to loot Forty Larch Hill Road instead of Forty Birch Hill. Perhaps she wanted Forty Birch Hill Road in Daltonville, instead of Dalton Centre. The possibilities for such an error in this section are myriad. And I suppose," he added reflectively, "if one stubbornly sought a brown paper package, one could doubtless unearth such an object in any given house, anywhere!"

"But it's crazy! What would Mrs. Mink *want* with it?" Harriman demanded.

"Of course, there's always a strong chance that she's a kleptomaniac," Leonidas returned, "with an irresistible yen for small brown paper packages."

"But it's *fishy!*" Harriman persisted. "It's—which turn do I take here?"

"Left. M'yes," Leonidas nodded, "how aptly you sum it all up! Fishy. M'yes, indeed. I concur. That incredible car, and those incredible giants—left again here, please."

"It all sounds to me," Harriman said, "like that god-awful radio thing my aunt listens to religiously every evening—by the way, I've been living with her since October. Lillian Rumford on Great Oak Road. Where I picked you up. I'm being broken into her late husband's insurance business. Well, anyway, this serial she listens to is about a fellow named Haseltine."

"Oh?" Leonidas said blandly. "Really?"

"*You'd* never hear it, I'm sure," Harriman said almost apologetically. "It's hardly your type. Begins with sirens and machine guns, and a sort of voice of doom saying '*HASELTINE!* HAS-EL-TINE to the RES-CUE!' Then all hell breaks loose. Well, this business sounds to me like so much Haseltine—now where?"

"Just up ahead," Leonidas told him. "By that iron gate."

Harriman looked at the massively ornate outlines of Balderston Hall, and whistled.

"Wow, what a thing!" he said. "Looks like a movie director's notion of a tycoon's palace of the Nineties, doesn't it? Iron gingerbread—and my God, what a hideous collection of stuff strewn around!"

His derisive gesture included the iron figure of a Negro jockey, which served as a hitching post by the gate, the iron stags halfway up the wide lawn, and the iron grapeleaf benches and table next to an iron fountain in which dolphins fought with cherubs.

"If anyone ever thought of making an iron wedding cake," Leonidas said, "I feel sure it would resemble this house. But unless I'm so late that Inga's soufflé has fallen by the wayside, I shall have an excellent dinner. I try to keep that point in mind, and never, never look at the décor any more than I have to. Harriman, I'm most grateful. If I may be of any assistance to you at any time, drop in on me at Forty Birch Hill. Very likely we'll be able to find some new type of insurance which someone has forgotten to sell me!"

He thought as he strode quickly up the walk that he really should have paused long enough to take in Fenwick's copy of the *Dalton Evening Chronicle*, reposing in the iron hand of the hitching post boy, but he was now so late that every second counted. He well knew Fenwick's opinion of tardy guests.

The front door was open, and Leonidas entered, assuming that Thor, the butler, would be waiting for him in the hall.

"I'm afraid that I came away hurriedly, without my hat and coa—oh."

Leonidas paused when he realized that he was talking to himself. Probably Thor, after opening the door for him, had dashed out to the kitchen to give Inga the glad tidings that their guest had finally arrived.

But Fenwick would, as usual, be in the library, that gloomy, mahogany-panelled room whose magnificent collection of books was so forbiddingly glassed in that Leonidas never even dared ask to hold one of the treasures in his hand.

"Balderston, my dear fellow, I *do* regret—"

He began his sentence as he crossed the library's threshold, and stopped it as his foot touched the antique Kabistan by the doorway.

Fenwick was, as usual, in the library.

Fenwick was lying on the Bokhara, his head in a pool of blood.

There would be no need to dash across the room, bend down, and investigate that still form to be assured that Fenwick was certainly dead, and that he had certainly met a violent death.

Leonidas, with a feeling of having suddenly been turned to stone, continued to stand in the doorway.

Somewhere inside of him, a voice as ominous as the one which introduced Haseltine on the radio kept saying the same thing, over and over and over.

"There'd be a corpse, of course. A man of distinction. A Corpse. A Man of Distinction."

4

AFTER WHAT SEEMED LIKE HOURS, the ominous voice mercifully stopped.

But another, shriller voice immediately took its place and began to scream out a horrible, factual statement.

"Killed with that paperweight you gave him! Killed with that paperweight you gave him! Killed with that paperweight you gave him!"

Leonidas slowly stepped across the Kabistan and, almost without being aware of his action, sat down heavily in an enormous red leather armchair.

Perhaps he had never been able to summon up any positive emotions toward Fenwick Balderston before, but he was certainly feeling them now. No one deserved this brutal sort of death. Certainly Fenwick didn't.

It dawned on Leonidas suddenly that he was still tensely gripping the little brown paper package with both hands. He let it drop into his lap while he cleaned his pince-nez and put them on. The familiar gesture seemed to soothe him and make him feel better, and he began to attempt to sort out some of the wild thoughts that had been racing through his mind.

There lay Fenwick, there beyond him lay the paperweight which he himself had given the man. It was beyond any peradventure of a doubt the blunt instrument which had been used to kill him, and to inflict those ugly wounds on his head.

The paperweight itself was a miniature bust of Shakespeare, perhaps five inches tall, and made of iron. Fenwick had admired the thing, the gift of some Meredith Academy group many years ago, and Leonidas had promptly given it to him with some lighthearted comment about adding to Balderston Hall's collection of miscellaneous ironmongery.

When? Leonidas shook his head. A year or more ago, following one of the meetings of the Dalton Collectors' Club at his house.

Could he prove that? Could he prove that the paperweight had been in Fenwick's possession all that time, that he himself had not brought it when he came here tonight?

There were so many ghastly little Shakespearean gift tidbits in his own study that Mrs. Mullet would probably be unable to differentiate between them, or to give any positive evidence on his behalf in court. The top of Fenwick's desk, in the corner, was an untidy litter of miniature busts of almost everyone who ever had merited a miniature bust, and a lot who hadn't. The overflow of his collection covered two other table tops and several shelves. Leonidas doubted if Thor or Inga would know whether or not this little Shakespeare bust had been among the others.

And a murder weapon was after all a murder weapon, whether it was an antique flintlock pistol or a Malay kris, a vial that had once contained potassium cyanide, or a rolled-up copy of the *Saturday Evening Post* which had been utilized as a club. Its ownership, whether relevant to the crime or not, was of importance.

"In short," Leonidas murmured aloud, "he was killed with an object which originally belonged to me, which I will be very hard pressed to prove was a gift to him, and an object already in his possession."

Where were Thor and Inga? He looked over at the pull-bell rope, but he felt no need to walk across and tug at it. The couple clearly couldn't be here in the house now.

There was absolutely no alternative but for him to call the Dalton Hills police. He might as well pull himself together and get it over with.

But instead of marching grimly to the telephone on the desk, he leaned back in the red leather chair, closed his eyes, and conjured up the dialogue which would take place on the arrival of Dalton's Finest.

"So you found him lying here when you come, huh, and you called us right away, huh?"

"That is correct."

"Hey, Mike!"—or Bill, or Mack, or whoever. "Hey, lookit this little statue here, see? This's what done it. Hey, look—it's got a *name* engraved on it!"

"Yeah? What's it say?"

"Says—uh—'Leo-*ni*-das Witherall.' " They would mispronounce his first name, of course. All nonclassical scholars usually did.

"Oh, it does, does it? Well, Mr. Witherall, what you got to say?"

"I gave that to Mr. Balderston a year or more ago."

"Oh, you *did?*" Rising inflection. "Well, Mr. Witherall, I guess you won't mind none if we ask you a few questions, like. When'd you come here, huh?"

"About twenty minutes or a quarter to eight. I can't be

exact. I was late. Mr. Harriman of Great Oak Road, who brought me in his car, could perhaps tell you more accurately."

"He picked you up at your house, huh?"

And that, Leonidas thought ruefully, was where it would begin to tear.

How could he say it?

"Er—not *exactly* at my home, Officer. I happened by the merest chance to be huddled on Mr. Harriman's car floor, and he very graciously gave me a lift."

Suppose that he did say just that. The police would only retort with the obvious question.

"What was you doing there on his car floor, huh, Mr. Witherall?"

"I was eluding a large group, including two giants who were pursuing me—yes, Officer, you heard. I said giants. They came from an Atomic Age automobile in response to a whistle. They were chasing me because I had snatched a package of mine from a woman with a stovepipe hat who rose from the vicinity of my front door like something out of a Jack Horner pie—"

Leonidas sighed and thought wistfully of the admirable injunction cut deep into the granite portals of Meredith's Academy. "Tell the Truth," it said, "and Fear No Man." Generations of Meredith boys had faced the world full of anticipation and hope, confident that the truth was a sort of invisible armor to protect them from the slings and arrows of outrageous fortune. During his teaching days, he had been as dutifully vigorous as the next Meredith master in dinning that sentiment into the erring young. At the drop of a hat, he had intoned to them a sententious poem whose pièce de résistance was a couplet about truth having no exceptions.

It was almost a relief to find himself wondering, parenthetically and quite irrelevantly, what in the world had rhymed with "exceptions." Or, for that matter, what had rhymed with "truth." But before he became distracted with any of the tantalizing possibilities, he forced himself back to the problems at hand.

While he was categorically pro-truth, here was one of those idiotic situations in which he could not possibly adhere to the truth. Harriman, an amiable fellow with no axes to grind, had barely been able to swallow his fantastic little narrative. With some justification, Harriman classified it with Haseltine.

How would the police classify it?

Leonidas shuddered at the thought.

And since Fenwick had so very recently met his death, his own whereabouts—say since seven o'clock that evening—were not without considerable significance.

But he simply could *not* tell the truth. While no one could disprove his story, no one was going to believe a word of it, either.

And any credible-sounding tale he might improvise on the spur of the moment would ultimately be ripped apart by the police. They might believe him implicitly at first, but they would disprove every word later.

And to keep silent would of course be completely fatal. Everyone would inevitably assume the worst if he refused point-blank to sum up his actions from the time he left his own house until he arrived here.

" 'Circumstantially implicated, backed by fate into a

43

corner—'" Leonidas murmured, quoting his own flippant words about Haseltine's projected dilemmas. "M'yes, m'yes, indeed!"

He turned and stared down at the still figure on the Bokhara.

One advantage in having written so many versions of this sort of scene was an ability to notice the details essential to fiction. He would hazard a guess that Fenwick had been sitting in his chair, that the paperweight had been smashed against his head several times by someone standing behind him, someone whose presence he hadn't suspected, or else someone whom he had no cause to suspect. The blows had been forceful enough to cause Fenwick to topple and fall from his chair.

Somewhere in the files at home in his study, he had several medically expert résumés on why bodies toppled this way or that way. While the technicalities always eluded him between manuscripts, Fenwick had fallen as he should if hit by what his files referred to as "Head Blow B." The first smash had killed him. The additional blows only indicated a display of uncontrolled fury on the part of the basher.

There was nothing in the picture before him to alter his long-standing opinion that the quick, efficient bash with some handy object snatched from the scene was the deadliest and most intelligent of murder methods. Guns jammed, knives required a certain passing acquaintance with anatomy, poisons reacted so unpredictably with certain types of individuals. All demanded elaborate planning, of which traces could always be unearthed by some dogged detective-equivalent of Sergeant MacCobble. The basher presented one with a fait accompli, courteously

44

left behind the weapon involved, and dared you to figure it out from there.

Could Inga and Thor have had anything to do with it?

In fictional murders it was tacitly considered unsporting to accuse the servants—at least, he mentally amended, in the non-gutty school where people still had servants. But in factual murders, a psychopathic cleaning woman or a mentally insecure grass-cutter seemed to turn up quite regularly as the murderers who had battered their respective employers to death. He could recall the newspaper headlines from at least three such affairs in the last few years.

But Inga and Thor adored Fenwick, and they were handsomely paid. Throughout the war years they had resisted such lures as managing the employees' restaurants at the Dalton Nut and Bolt Company and the Dalton Tap and Dye Works, which between them had siphoned off most of the county's competent servants. Considering their intimate knowledge of Fenwick and their familiarity with the house, there would seem so many easier ways for them to have done away with him. A cord stretched across the highly polished surface of those treacherous front hall stairs, for example. Or some sinister manipulation of the rungs of the tall library ladder. Or Inga could merely have dropped a snidget of arsenic into the bouillabaisse, or laced a batch of marzipan cookies with cyanide.

Leonidas shook his head and decided that by and large it would be quite unreasonable to assume that the couple would spring a sneak attack on Fenwick now, after living with him all these years in manifest contentment and satisfaction. A bash, moreover, seemed inconsistent with the

45

way in which their minds worked. A bash would not appeal to their—how could it be summed up?—their intricately-garnished-hors-d'oeuvres type of thinking.

He got up suddenly from his armchair and made his way through the center hall to the vast, old-fashioned kitchen.

Dozens of opened oysters sat in their shells on a block of ice in a wash tub, ready to be transferred to their beds of crushed ice. A green salad was in a bowl, ready to be tossed. Vegetables were ready for the pressure cooker, an orange sauce was simmering in a double boiler, wild rice was steeping in a bowl of lukewarm water, and through the transparent door of the warming oven, Leonidas could see two ducks proudly sitting. A mousse mold was packed in ice in a pail near the door, and a tray of petits fours was carefully covered with wax paper.

Thor and Inga had certainly been on the premises until very recently, and working like two little beavers, to boot.

The only conclusion Leonidas could draw after surveying that array of food brought a thoughtful frown to his face, and caused him to swing around and stroll through the long narrow pantry into the dining room, where he snapped on the light.

The sudden brilliance of the ornate cut-glass chandelier made him blink, and he automatically turned his head away from the center of the room.

A fire was laid in the white marble fireplace, the red plush draperies were drawn at the windows, and the carved rosewood chairs with the dark red velvet seats were placed with their usual mathematical precision against the chair rail of the dark red wallpaper.

And the white damask-covered dining table had its

usual opulent assortment of shining crystal, and heavy silver, and gold-crusted Lenox.

And—it was set for three guests!

Leonidas smiled and glanced back into the pantry at a tray containing a decanter of sherry.

And three glasses!

"I thought," Leonidas murmured, "that three dozen oysters was rather a lot of oysters when two dozen would have sufficed. M'yes, indeed! What a gentle, non-gutty clew to indicate the presence of another guest!"

He returned to the library, circled around the Bokhara, and peered at the tooled leather engagement pad on Fenwick's mahogany desk.

But all it said was, "L.W. Dinner."

Was this third guest a sudden, afterthought addition to the party, someone invited so late that Fenwick, a most methodical man, had no time to note down the fact of his coming?

Ordinarily, Leonidas thought as he played with his pince-nez, he wouldn't give Fenwick credit for any such impulsive or spontaneous action as inviting a dinner guest at the very last mo—

The pince-nez fell from his hand as someone beat a sudden tattoo on the front door knocker.

"T HOR!"

A sudden roar went up as someone noisily entered the front hall.

Leonidas stifled his immediate impulse to flee through the stained-glass window that led outdoors to a terrace. He had run away once that evening, and once was enough. Sooner or later, he would have to face this thing, and he might as well start in becoming accustomed to it.

"Thor! I say, damn it!" The man's voice rose to an irritated bellow. "Thor!"

He'll come marching into the library now, Leonidas thought to himself, just as I did!

But the heavy, determined footsteps stomped through the center hall, directly past the open library door, and out to the kitchen, from which more strident bellowings arose.

"Thor! I've got a cheese—"

Unquestionably this was the other guest tardily arriving with gifts, Leonidas decided as he walked over to the red leather chair and picked up his package. While his only present feeling for that small, flat, brown paper-wrapped object was one of marked loathing, it was all he possessed in the nature of tangible proof to substantiate that idiot story he was shortly going to have to start telling, and—what would be harder—sticking to in the face of all jeering opposition.

Something glittered and caught his eye as he moved away from the chair, something that had fallen behind the red leather seat cushion, something he had completely failed to notice for all that he had literally sat upon it for some ten minutes.

Reaching down, he pulled out a small green leather pocketbook which fastened with a shining chromium clasp in the shape of an overgrown modernistic beetle.

Leonidas raised his eyebrows quizzically.

A woman's pocketbook, stuffed in behind one of Fenwick's library chair cushions?

And not, to judge from its jaunty outward appearance, anything which belonged to one of Fenwick's more than middle-aged contemporaries. This was a gay, youthful pocketbook.

He was starting to open it when the bellowings for Thor became mingled with another loud pounding sound, rather like someone battering against a door.

"Damn it, Thor, where the hell *are* you?"

There were more batterings and poundings and bangings, and more angry questions from the noisy visitor.

Slipping both his package and the little green bag under his arm, Leonidas stepped quietly out into the hall and crossed over into the dining room, still brightly illuminated by the cut-glass chandelier which he had forgotten to snap off.

He paused for a moment at the doorway to the darkened pantry, and then tiptoed inside far enough so that he could observe what was taking place in the kitchen.

All the thumping and banging seemed to be occurring on the far side of a closed door set in the opposite wall between a square, awkward-looking electric refrigerator

49

of the Twenties, and a pair of vintage soapstone laundry tubs of the Nineties.

The newcomer, a short stocky man with a completely bald head, was apparently trying to open the door from the kitchen side.

"For God's sakes, Thor," he paused long enough in his exertions to yell out in exasperated tones, "what the hell are you doing in there, anyway? Who jammed this damn thing?"

He had quite a lot more to say before he finally managed, with the aid of a great deal of panting and jerking, to open the door.

Thor emerged, looking shorter and more wispish than ever beside Inga's vast bulk.

"Inga's in there, *too?* For the love of all that's holy, what *are* you two doing in that wine closet? What's that?" He gave them practically no chance to answer. "*Locked* in? Locked *in?* I never heard of anything so damned silly in all my life! *Why?* Why lock yourselves in a wine closet? What's that? A spring lock? Well, you certainly must've known by now that it was a spring lock, didn't you? Here, take this Roquefort I brought—it's a perfect beauty! *Locked* in the wine closet! My God!"

Inga retained her usual wooden expression throughout his vehement monologue, but Thor looked both embarrassed and unhappy.

"But, sir, you see," he cleared his throat, "we were *locked* in—"

"*If* you remember," the bald man interrupted acidly, "*I* just let you out! *I* know you were locked in! How'd the door get so jammed?"

"That's what I mean, Doctor Fell. Somebody *locked* us in!"

"You're certainly not trying to insinuate that Fenwick Balderston has taken to playing April Fool tricks at his age, I hope? Someone locked you in! What's the matter, are you *drunk?*"

From his vantage point, Leonidas could hear Doctor Fell's suspicious sniffing.

"No, sir!" Thor said firmly. "We got locked in. By Mr. Witherall, it must have been."

"By *who?*"

Except for his grammar, Leonidas thought, Doctor Fell had taken those words right out of his own mouth.

"Mr. Witherall, sir. He was expected here for dinner. He—"

"Who *is* he? What's he *do?*" Fell broke in.

"A friend of Mr. Balderston's, sir. A director of our bank. But—"

"Oh, banker, huh? Now why the hell should a banker lock you two up in the wine closet? He tight?"

"*We* don't know, sir." Thor returned. "Mr. Balderston called out to me as I was going through the hall, and he said he saw Mr. Witherall coming, and he'd let him in. I heard him come in, and then a few minutes later I was in the wine closet, and Inga stepped in to ask me about something, and then someone slammed that door on us. We couldn't get out. We tried to. We—"

"Probably boiled to the gills," Fell said. "Why didn't you yell?"

"We did! But Mr. Balderston didn't hear us, and so we decided not to yell any more until someone came near

51

enough so as they'd hear us, and then you called my name, and we yelled back. That's how it was, Doctor Fell!"

Leonidas nodded.

That was how it was.

After killing Fenwick, the murderer had started out the back way, had with great good fortune found both servants in an ideal position to be immobilized, and—being nobody's fool—had taken instant advantage of the situation.

The discovery of that spring lock's presence had probably been cause for a brief moment of jubilation. Not that any hastily improvised wedge wouldn't have served him almost as well, had the door been devoid of any locks or bolts.

All in all, Leonidas thought, the murderer had been admirably successful in his primary objective of keeping the servants from stumbling on Fenwick's body until after he had departed. Whatever clamor they might make in the closet wouldn't matter a whit.

"How long you been *in* there?" Fell demanded, comparing his watch with the kitchen clock.

"Oh, a *long* while, sir! Mr. Witherall came at ten past seven, and it's nearly ten past eight, now."

"My God—and Fenwick hasn't been out here to find you? Why in hell didn't you *bang?*"

"We banged, sir. For quite a long time," Thor told him. "I think that's how the door got jammed so bad. From Inga's kicking at it. But if he heard, Mr. Balderston didn't pay any attention. We didn't expect him to. We—"

"*Didn't* expect him to? For God's sakes, why *not?*"

"He never comes out here, sir. Never. Does he, Inga?"

"Never. Not when the boiler blows up, even," Inga said with pride. "That is our agreement. Never no bother in my kitchen, never no coming in, no matter for what reason why. Always best that way. No—"

"When do we eat?" Fell helped himself to a celery heart. "My plane," he continued with his mouth full, "was an hour late from Chicago. I'm starved."

Walking over to the tray of petits fours, he picked one up, looked at it critically, and then tossed it back on the tray. After pawing over and discarding two more, he finally found one to his liking, and over-optimistically stuffed it into his mouth as one bite.

Up till now, Doctor Fell's face had been more or less hidden by Inga's wooden profile, and the upper part of the coffee grinder on the pantry wall. His stroll over to the cakes gave Leonidas his first real chance to get an unobstructed picture of the man.

He didn't like what he could see above and below and between those bulging cheeks—beady, close-set eyes, a broad flat nose, a thick-lipped mouth whose outlines were obscured by a toothbrush mustache, and several chins.

He didn't like Doctor Fell's brown suit with the wide chalk stripe, or his matching brown shirt, or his apoplectic, hand-painted necktie. Doubtless a creation of the Allbright Brothers, Leonidas decided.

Whoever laughingly referred to himself as Doctor Fell's dentist, furthermore, should be ridden out of his profession on the end of a rail. On second thought, Leonidas conceded charitably, possibly those teeth had been cared for—and supplied by—some generous old forty niner whose pockets were stuffed to overflowing with golden nuggets.

53

The lines of Brown's old poem floated through his mind:

> "I do not love thee, Doctor Fell,
> The reason why I cannot tell.
> But this alone I know full well,
> I do not love thee, Doctor Fell."

On the whole, Leonidas reflected as he watched the doctor wolf down two more cakes, he was going to resent telling his story to Fell more than to the police. While the latter might at least accord him some faint vestige of respect as a Dalton taxpayer, this man would probably never permit him to finish a sentence.

"My God!" The doctor nearly choked to death as he tried to eat his cake and yell at Thor at the same time. "Don't!"

"Don't what, sir?"

Thor paused with his right hand on the handle of the ancient electric refrigerator. In his left hand, he was holding the Roquefort cheese which Doctor Fell had brought with him.

"Don't try to stuff that cheese in *there!*" Fell ordered. "It's too full! Put it out in the other chest, the old ice chest, where there's plenty of room!"

"Yes, sir."

Thor didn't seem to notice anything at all out of the ordinary in the doctor's command, but Leonidas began to smile.

Thor hadn't opened the refrigerator when the doctor started to yell at him.

How, then, would Fell know with such certainty that there was no room for his cheese?

Leonidas's smile widened.

The doctor certainly didn't appear to him to be gifted with the second sight!

Therefore—

Leonidas started to tiptoe quietly back into the dining room.

Therefore, if Fell was so intimately acquainted with the contents of that refrigerator, Fell must have looked inside.

When?

Not in the interval during which Leonidas had been watching him from the pantry.

Not before that, when Fell first entered the kitchen, while he was screaming and howling for Thor. There could hardly have been time enough for the man to have examined the contents of two refrigerators before he set to work trying to free Thor and Inga from the confines of the wine closet.

Even admitting that Fell might have given a quick glance into the kitchen refrigerator, how could he have known the location—let alone the state of its contents—of this "other" chest, this "old ice chest" to which he referred so glibly?

The conclusion was obvious.

This was *not* Doctor Fell's first visit to the kitchen this evening!

Fell had been here earlier. He must have been here earlier.

That was why he had marched past the library door without stopping to speak to Fenwick. Fell knew that Fenwick was dead.

While it was somewhat premature to conclude that Fell was the murderer, Leonidas thought as he tiptoed across

55

the dining room, one might at least toy lightly with the question of whether Fell hadn't gone straight out to the kitchen with some definite intention of liberating Thor and Inga.

That was the eminently fair approach. That was merely *assuming* that he was the one who had locked them up in the first place.

"When he so very carefully planted in their minds the information that his plane was an hour late," Leonidas murmured to himself as he paused on the threshold of the center hall, "I wondered. M'yes, and when he gave them no chance to question *him* about anything. Always clipping them off in mid-air. M'yes, very neat!"

But because the doctor couldn't curb his impulse to give orders, he had given himself away.

To Leonidas's entire satisfaction, anyway, even though he felt sure that the Dalton police would probably place no significance whatsoever in the fact that a certain man knew that a certain cheese wouldn't fit into a certain refrigerator!

"Such non-gutty clews!" he mused regretfully.

It hardly seemed proper to draw inferences and conclusions from oysters and cheeses and old iceboxes and brown paper packages!

But thanks to oysters and a Roquefort cheese, he had found out enough to know that someone besides himself could be chosen as an alternate burnt offering, a potential suspect in the affair of Fenwick's murder.

Leonidas crossed the center hall, slipped into the library, and stood there for a moment.

While he knew much more now than he'd known only fifteen minutes before, his own position had deteriorated.

Not only was he circumstantially implicated, but he was now certain to be falsely accused. Thor's and Inga's strange conviction that it was he who had locked them up in the wine closet was going to tie in so handily with that paperweight of his!

He kept wishing that those fifty acres so necessary for the future growth and expansion of Meredith's Academy would stop haunting the recesses of his mind! Never would the miserly Mrs. Goldthwaite of Fairlawns bestow those acres, in a merry burst of generosity, on a publicized murder suspect. Never.

How might she react if a falsely accused suspect turned detective, and brilliantly solved an evil murder all by himself?

Whether or not her charitable instincts would be roused, the successful amateur detective assuredly stood more chance of wangling those precious acres than did any cringing suspect.

Leonidas knew perfectly well in his heart that ever since the advent of Doctor Fell, he had no intention other than that of girding his loins and following this business through by himself in the Haseltine manner. He knew that the only way to extricate himself was to continue finding out more. And more.

But the thought of those fifty acres gave his decision a certain status. They added just the requisite touch of Holy Crusade.

And one would never find out more and more when one was sitting on a cell cot in the Dalton Jail, playing gin rummy for matches with one's lawyer.

He took a last, unhurried look around Fenwick's library.

He had Doctor Fell to begin work with, and it was his firm intention to leave Balderston Hall at once, in a dignified and unhurried exit through the front door, and to start finding out who this Fell was, why he was here, and to check on that conveniently late Chicago plane.

There was that little green pocketbook to look into, too.

Probably it would be asking too much of fate to hope that somewhere in the shuffle, he might even discover why that woman in the stovepipe hat had chosen to steal his package.

He swung around suddenly and listened to the agitated voices now coming from the dining room—and rapidly coming nearer.

"Balderston himself!" Thor was saying. *"Didn't* he send you out to find us, Doctor Fell?"

Leonidas saw the swift evaporation of his plan for an unhurried exit through the front door.

Gripping the brown paper package and the green pocketbook, he slid behind the long brown velvet curtains drawn in front of the stained-glass French window that led out on the terrace.

"But I thought of course Mr. Balderston sent you out to find us, sir!" There was real concern in Thor's voice. *"I* didn't understand you hadn't even *seen* him! *I* thought he sent you! Why, I'd have come at once to see him if I'd only known—"

They were crossing the hall, now.

Leonidas decided that he was probably making a magnificent silhouette of himself for the outside world to see, but he would regretfully have to remain behind the curtains until the room was empty. Then he would leave unobtrusively by the window.

And perhaps it was just as well for him to hear what took place when they discovered Fenwick.

Thor's anguished cry rang out, then Inga's blood-curdling scream, and then Fell's loud, futile shout of "Balderston!"

It was all a routine preface to a conversation and to reactions which Leonidas had written many, many times before.

Thor and Inga might be Haseltine's Faithful Frank and Lady Alicia's maid, Mario.

And Doctor Fell was the character who always, on first beholding the lifeless form of his great friend, swore his mightiest oath that the dastardly villain responsible for this foul deed would not go unpunished, that even if the task of tracking him down consumed the rest of his days, and led him—so to speak—from the rock-bound coast of Maine to the sunny shores of California, via Zanzibar, Ciudad Trujillo, Nova Zembla, or any other spots Leonidas could think of at the moment of writing—and could spell without getting up and consulting an atlas.

"What was the name again of that fellow who locked you up?" Fell demanded with just the proper amount of grimness. "That banker fellow?"

"Witherall. Mr. Leonidas Witherall."

Leonidas heard the sound of the desk phone's receiver being snatched up.

"Emergency!" Fell announced importantly. "Emergency! Police!"

Leonidas could hear the proper, impatient drumming of Fell's knuckles on the top of Fenwick's desk as he waited for the call to be put through.

"Dalton police? This is Doctor B. J. Fell speaking. I

am calling from the residence of Fenwick Balderston. I have just arrived here to find his servants locked up in a closet, and Mr. Balderston himself murdered. That's correct. Murdered. The servants say they were locked up by a Mr. Leonidas Witherall—that's correct. Did *he?* I assume that he must have. Thank you. Yes, I will see that nothing is touched or disturbed in any way until you get here."

Lucid, crisp, and to the point, Leonidas thought with approval. Just a deft flick of his wrist, and Doctor Fell had tossed him into the ring as Leading Contender for the title of Balderston Murder Suspect Number One.

No, those fifty acres would never be wangled for Meredith's until that criminal stigma on his name turned into a bright red, neon halo!

With growing concern, he listened to Fell's assurances to Thor that he would personally oversee everything, and that yes, yes, indeed, he would personally remain right here, right in the library until the arrival of the police.

That, Leonidas reflected, was an unfortunate development which he ought to have foreseen when he so blithely whipped in behind that curtain!

Fell's next comment sounded like a comparatively gentle suggestion, but it had an undertone of urgency which caused Leonidas to raise his eyebrows.

"Just you run along and take care of Inga, Thor! Just take her out of here and calm her down—yes, yes, I understand how broken up she is! You two shouldn't stay in here. Too harrowing for both of you. Just you two go somewhere else. *I'll* stay."

Which, literally translated, seemed to indicate that

Doctor Fell wished very much to be left alone in the library.

When the sound of Inga's convulsive weeping finally faded away, Leonidas very cautiously drew back the brown velvet curtain the fraction of a fraction of a quarter of an inch.

Through the hairline slit, he could see Fell bending over Fenwick's desk.

Running through Fenwick's personal checkbook?

No. Nor his letters, either.

Pamphlets?

*Pamp*hlets?

Leonidas asked himself *why* pamphlets?

But what Fell was examining with such avidity certainly *looked* like pamphlets, or small catalogues of some sort.

Leonidas frowned and wished that he dared to run the risk of moving the curtains while he put on his pince-nez.

Pamphlets? Catalogues?

His frown deepened, and he half-closed his eyes in his effort to bring into focus the objects of Fell's intense, almost frenzied examination.

Of course they couldn't possibly be pamphlets or catalogues, as they seemed to be! Why would Fell maneuver Thor out of the room in order to scrutinize those collectors' catalogues which Fenwick customarily kept in untidy little heaps on his desk? The very thought was absurd. Any member of the Dalton Collectors' Club had a bushel or two of similar items lying around his house. Anyone at all, Fell included, could achieve his own private bushel simply for the asking, or at most for a few cents' postage!

Despite the fact that they still kept looking like catalogues to Leonidas, he knew it simply couldn't be catalogues that Fell was still pawing through.

Haseltine, he thought enviously, never ran into this realistic type of misfortune. Haseltine, ever young and ever in the state which he described as The Pink, suffered neither from astigmatism nor myopia.

At the sound of footsteps in the hall, Fell dropped the catalogues—if they *were* catalogues—as if they were live coals.

By the time Thor appeared in the doorway, Fell was standing several yards from Fenwick's desk, looking down at the Bokhara.

As Thor stepped over the threshold, Leonidas noticed that he deliberately turned his head away from Fenwick's body.

Leonidas saw the man's quick start, and automatically reached his right hand back and caught at the handle of the French window.

He knew what Thor had seen.

It was what Haseltine—and everyone else in the world —invariably spotted when people were unwise enough to hide behind curtains.

The tips of his shoes!

Leonidas drew a long breath, and got out of the window just a split second before Thor and Fell came thundering toward him.

And he reached the terrace just in time to hear the shrieking siren of the Dalton police car—no, *all* the sirens of *all* the Dalton police cars! All the sirens in the world, in fact, suddenly seemed to be screaming on Kenilworth Road!

"Get him, Thor!" Fell shouted. "You get him! I'll tell the police to head—"

There would be no John L. Lewis to help him here, Leonidas thought as he started in desperation toward the cover of Fenwick's orchard. No conveniently parked car, no helpful Harriman at the spent end of the trail. And not just amused and slightly supercilious neighbors in at the kill!

This was the sort of thing which Faithful Frank was accustomed to refer to as The Real McCoy.

And Thor seemed even brisker on his feet than those giants back on Birch Hill Road.

Thor also knew the terrain, which made a vast difference.

There was no sense now in Leonidas's trying to recall just which piece of the assorted ironmongery on the lawn possessed a large hollow base, as Fenwick had once shown him. Even if he remembered it was the stag and not a greyhound, he couldn't use it as a hiding place, for Thor would know all about it, too!

He kept on doggedly toward the orchard, hoping piously that there'd be nothing in his way to trip him.

And Thor kept doggedly on behind.

And in the distance, over the wail of one shrill, persistent siren, came the sounds of a really seriously organized chase.

Leonidas found himself regretting that the octopus of fate had got in all its beneficent licks earlier in the evening.

He had far greater need of it, right now!

There was a sudden cry and a thudding noise behind him—Thor had tripped?

Thor had!

But Leonidas's sense of relief was very short-lived.

For one of the police, obviously fleeter of foot than his colleagues, had apparently arrived on the scene just as Thor fell, and was vigorously taking up where Thor had stopped.

His hand was already gripping Leonidas's elbow.

Gripping his elbow—but not stopping him!

Gripping his elbow—and steering—actually *steering* him!

"To the right!" a deep voice said in his ear. "Through that gate, here—quick!"

Leonidas told himself that it was he who'd tripped and fallen. Not Thor.

He was dazed, dreaming, suffering hallucinations—of course he was!

No pursuing cop at this point was going to shove him through a gate in Fenwick's back garden wall, stuff him into a car, and drive him away from all this!

But when the car door, in closing, caught and pinched his finger, he realized that it was all indisputably real.

"The octopus of fate!" Leonidas used up his last spoonful of breath as the car jumped away from the garden gate as if it were jet-propelled. "Thank you, Harriman. Thank you again!"

"I'm not Harriman."

Leonidas whipped on his pince-nez and surveyed the driver of the coupé. He was a young man, lean and spare, and he wore shell-rimmed glasses. His hair was cropped close in a crew haircut, and like Leonidas, he was wearing a dinner jacket.

"Er—so you're not," Leonidas said as the car seemed

to streak from Dalton Hills to Daltonville to Daltondale in one easy jump. "But I dare say you have a name?"

"Shaver. Philip Shaver."

"Thank you, Mr. Shaver," Leonidas said. "Er—I believe you heard some faint cries of 'Murder!' back there at Balderston Hall?"

"Uh-huh."

"And you don't believe in signs—I mean, in cries?"

"I know *you* didn't kill Balderston." Shaver was entering Pomfret now.

"Indeed? And why not, may I ask?"

"I saw him before you did," Shaver returned.

"And—er—you know who did kill him?"

"Yes," Shaver said. "A woman."

6

AN ILLUMINATED SIGN flashed by.

"LEAVING BEAUTIFUL POMFRET," it said. "Founded 1699. The Little Town with the Big Futu—"

If it had said Beautiful Oz or Beautiful Shangrila, Leonidas reflected, he wouldn't have been at all surprised.

As they sped into Carnavon, Shaver said with finality, "*That's* why."

"Er—why what?"

"Why I conked that character who was chasing you in Uncle Fenwick's garden. I knew you didn't kill him. But if you want to know the truth, I'd be the hell of a lot happier if I knew who you were! I mean, what're you dressed up like Shakespeare for? Is it fancy dress or something? What's the idea of the false beard?"

"Incredible as it may perhaps seem to you," Leonidas said, "it's quite genuine—and please feel quite free to make a test case and give it a brisk tug, if you so desire. I am Leonidas Witherall of Dalton—"

The coupé slewed to a stop on the busy six-lane highway on the outskirts of Carnavon.

"Are you Bill Shakespeare?" Shaver demanded. "Bill Shakespeare of Meredith's?"

"M'yes. I—"

"Yaaa!" Shaver leaned back against the seat and emitted a triumphant war whoop which would have done credit to a battle-bound Apache, and which very nearly cost Leonidas the use of his left ear. "The Brain! Yaaaaa!"

"To—er—coin a phrase," Leonidas said, "how's that again?"

"That's what they used to call you at St. Luke's Academy in my day, some ten years ago," Shaver said. "The Brain. You'd bring over those scrawny little Meredith football teams—skinny, popeyed Sinatras! Pushovers! We never knew how it happened, but some time during the game, you'd whisper a few words to some pitiful little ten-year-old, and send him in as quarterback—and that was all, brother, but all! When the smoke cleared away, Meredith's had somehow *won!*"

"Ah, that was during our—er—frail era," Leonidas said reminiscently. "In the interests of self-preservation, we were often forced to utilize a certain amount of guile—"

"Guile? It was more like black magic! Look, sir, five minutes ago, before I knew who you were, I was all set to dump you by the wayside if you turned out to be what I susp—well, you see, I thought that beard was a fake, and you were another! But now—hell, if you could master-mind those Meredith teams, you can master-mind anything! Even this mess I've got myself into—look, did you ever find the truth so crazy that you knew no one'd ever believe a word of it if you told it to 'em?"

"Mr. Shaver," Leonidas said gravely, "permit me to shake your hand! Thank you. Er—just what is this crazy truth which so distresses you? Does it, I trust, have to do with your Uncle Fenwick?"

"He's not a real uncle, sir. He and my father were at college together, and I was always forced to call him

Uncle. When he took me into the bank, he seemed to expect me to keep it up, so I did. I work for the Dalton Safe Deposit and Trust, you see."

"Do you, indeed?" Leonidas said. "So do I. At least, I'm a director. But—"

"*Are* you?" Shaver interrupted in surprise. "Honestly? Good God! Well, let this be a lesson to you, Shaver-boy. First thing tomorrow morning, you *read* those lists on that bulletin board!"

"I don't recall," Leonidas said, "ever having seen you in the bank."

"I'm the new general assistant. You wouldn't. I'm not on display. I'm more in the bowels of the joint. They call it," Shaver said, "learning the banking business from the ground up. I rush around putting refills of paper cups in the water cooler, and I oil typewriters—and sometimes, about once a week, I'm sent out on a very, very, very important mission!"

"Oh?"

"After exhaustive briefing," Shaver continued with more than a touch of irony in his voice, "I walk carefully around the corner to Atkinson's Pharmacy and get a large mocha malted in a paper container for Uncle Fenwick. One-third coffee, two-thirds chocolate, and three large straws, please."

"M'yes, the practical side, as it is termed," Leonidas said. "Would it make your lot seem brighter, I wonder, to know that junior masters at Meredith's spend much of their time making and dispensing ink, pasting pages into Latin grammars, and trying to attach orphan overshoes to likely sized feet? Er—I have rather a strong chronological sense, Shaver, as well as an outsize curiosity. Exactly how did you happen to be on the scene and in a position to rescue me, back at Balderston Hall?"

"Oh, I'd been watching around the place a long time," Shaver told him casually. "Say, do you know it's getting colder? Aren't you freezing?" He leaned over and snapped on the car heater. "Feels to me like snow!"

Leonidas reminded him that it was November. "Late November, I grant you, but none the less November—er —about Balderston Hall?" he added with rising inflection.

Shaver lighted a cigarette. "Well, Shakespeare, I'd been on the terrace trying to peek in, and up on the kitchen window ledges, and I'd even crawled up on some of those iron balconies out back. But it's the hell of a place to see into—everything drawn, and draped, and curtained! And then finally I saw your silhouette at the library window, against the glass—those draperies have a light lining, or something, I guess, because you stood out like a sore thumb!"

"I rather suspected that I might." Leonidas turned the collar of his dinner jacket up around his neck. "You know, it *does* seem much colder!"

"It *is!* Well, I watched you cut and run," Shaver continued, "and I heard all that hue and cry, and decided it was time I beat it, too. I knew you hadn't killed Uncle Fenwick, whoever you were, and I wanted to find out what you might know, so I conked that character chasing you—and here we are!"

"While it may seem like a most elementary question," Leonidas said, "just why *were* you watching around the place and generally peering into windows?"

"Because when I went there, around quarter past seven

or so, there was Uncle Fenwick on the library floor, dead!" Shaver returned. "Murdered! And I wasn't going to be the fall guy who called the cops! I don't mean to seem callous, but there certainly wasn't anything *I* could do about him, and well—I *couldn't* call the cops! First of all, that business at the bank—"

He paused.

"A shortage, perhaps?" Leonidas inquired.

Shaver shook his head. "I don't know. But something's wrong. A bank examiner dropped in unexpectedly today —and we'd had one only last week. No one said anything to me, mind you—this is all my guesswork. But I think there *is* some problem, and I'm pretty sure it concerns Fergus McLean."

"The cashier?" Leonidas asked. "The one who looks as if he were about to lay a cornerstone, or dedicate a solemn monument? He overawes me to such an extent that I customarily cash my checks at the Dalton Savings, down the street."

"That's McLean. But he wouldn't have overawed a flea, this afternoon. Comrade McLean," Shaver said, "had as bad a case of the jitters as I ever saw. No one mentioned it, no one said anything about anything. Everyone was very proper and deadpan. But just before I left, I got a message from Uncle Fenwick. He asked if I'd come to dinner at his house tonight—"

"*What?*" Leonidas put on his pince-nez and stared at Shaver. "To*night?*"

So the third place at the table had not been set for Doctor Fell?

"Yes, and would I please drop by early. I've got the note in my wallet—want to see it?"

70

He passed it over, and snapped on the dome light long enough for Leonidas to read the brief invitation written on the bank's stationery, and unquestionably in Fenwick's own handwriting. It was even dated, and timed.

"Royal command," Shaver remarked. "I wrote back a polite acceptance at once, of course, and then went and broke the other date I'd made for tonight. Do you know Uncle Fenwick at all well? I don't," he went on without giving Leonidas time to answer. "I just saw him with the family when I was a kid. He's never asked me to dinner before in the two months I've been working at the bank! And following on the heels of that bank examiner—well, I didn't like any part of it!"

"You mean," Leonidas said thoughtfully, "that if there *is* something wrong at the bank, you suspect that the blame will be placed on you? That perhaps Fenwick intended to broach the topic at dinner? I see. But—forgive my phrasing this so baldly—d'you really feel that you are in a position of sufficient authority, so to speak, to have anything very serious pinned on you?"

"Oh, I'm under no illusions as to where I rate in that outfit!" Shaver said. "Even the cleaning woman and the cat have seniority. But—this is the point—I do a little bit of everything for everybody. That's the process called 'Trying you out to find your proper niche,' you know. And this last week, McLean's given me reams of stuff to copy for him. Figures and accounts. It occurs to me there's a lot that *looks* like my handiwork!"

"But people will certainly know that you were merely copying for McLean!"

"People will know just exactly whatever McLean chooses to tell them!" Shaver said. "And there I am! And

71

McLean has some relation who expected to get this job of mine, according to the bank grapevine—someone who is still very available if I don't pan out! McLean's always been decent enough to me, but there's always been an undercurrent—oh, it's all in the air! I haven't any proof! I haven't any proof of anything, Shakespeare!"

Leonidas reflected for a moment. He had known junior masters at Meredith's to grow haggard and lose weight over trivia like misplaced Form marks, and to translate his own cheerful good-morning greeting to them as the direst warning of their imminent dismissal. Unquestionably there was a touch of that sort of thing in Shaver's suspicions—but perhaps, under the circumstances, he was quite justified in having suspicions.

On his mental list, Leonidas inscribed the name of Fergus McLean under that of Doctor Fell.

"You went to Fenwick's around quarter past seven, you say—where were Thor and Inga? Didn't you see any sign of servants? Didn't you hear any noises?"

"No. I hadn't been to Balderston Hall since I was—oh, thirteen or fourteen! Before mother and dad died. I kept thinking that there ought to be servants around—there always used to be droves of 'em. But then after I found Uncle Fenwick, they somehow slipped my mind. I can't remember why—but it seems to me for some reason or other, I assumed they'd rushed off for a doctor. I—then I—then—"

He stopped short.

"Did you just go in, and then go out?" Leonidas asked.

"Yes. This—look, this is where the crazy angles begin to creep in. I saw Uncle Fenwick—and all of a sudden, this bank examiner business that I'd been worrying about seemed to blow up inside of me. I had a lot of pictures of myself under bright spotlights, with cops waggling their fingers in my face and yelling what did I do with that money missing from the bank, and why did I kill Fenwick—and someone was winding up to belt me again with a length of rubber hose. Third degree stuff—you know what I mean?"

"M'yes." Leonidas did not trouble to add that he had written every word of it as a typical corpse-viewing reaction some several thousand times.

"Well, I started out of that library like a bat out of hell. I—I—"

Shaver stopped short again.

"Er—yes?" Leonidas said encouragingly.

"Well, I—oh, what's the use! You won't believe it! I know you won't!"

"I can hardly disbelieve you," Leonidas pointed out, "until I have some faint indication of what not to believe. Now this is entirely beside the point, but it may—er— give you courage. I used to have a paper boy who came in a Cadillac, with a chauffeur. D'you find that hard to accept?"

"Not," Shaver said, "if you can explain why!"

"He is a paper boy," Leonidas said, "because his father was a paper boy, and believes that being a paper boy is the first rung on the ladder of success, and a prerequisite for the proper understanding of the value of money. But the task of getting the child to his work fell on his mother, who is only moderately Spartan. So whenever she overslept, or whenever the weather looked at all threatening,

73

she sent him forth in the Cadillac, with the chauffeur. Some seemingly bizarre statements, in short, may have the simplest explanations!"

"Mine," Shaver said with conviction, "won't!"

"Some time ago," Leonidas decided to try another approach, "you said that it was a woman who was responsible for Fenwick's death. Er—what led you to that conclusion, may I ask?"

"Well, that's the crazy part. When I went into the library—I'd just walked right into the house because the front door was open—well, on the table in the front hall—"

He stopped and drew a long breath.

"All right!" he said in tones almost as belligerent as Doctor Fell's. "You asked for it! On the front hall table —*there was a monkey in a red coat eating a Delicious apple!* And beside it—there was a round quart box of ice cream! And *now* what have you got to say?"

"I should say," Leonidas told him gently, "that you'd been privileged to view far more interesting objects on Fenwick's hall table than ever caught my eye. Er—why should a monkey in a red coat eating a Delicious apple, and a quart of ice cream cause you to assume that the murderer was a woman? Don't you really think," he added with sincerity, "that's rather an *unusual* deduction?"

"No, damn it, I don't! There was a mink coat on the chair by the table!"

"Indeed!"

"And when I came hotfooting it out of that library, damn it, they were all gone! Everything was gone—the

74

monkey, the quart of ice cream, the mink coat! There wasn't a trace of the lot of 'em! And I tell you, they *were* there when I went into that room! *Now* d'you see why I couldn't have called the cops, even if there hadn't been this other mess about the bank? Can you see the Dalton cops—or *any* cops *any*where, or anyone *else*—believing *one* single word of it?"

"I wonder," Leonidas said as he thoughtfully twirled his pince-nez, "what flavor."

Shaver groaned.

"I knew it! *You* don't believe me! You just think I'm making it up as I go along!"

"While we will doubtless never know," Leonidas said, "I hope from the bottom of my heart that it was pistachio. Oysters, Roquefort cheese—m'yes, unquestionably, it really *should* have been pistachio! Was it? I wish I knew!"

"I do hope," Shaver said with irony, "that such a vital little problem won't keep you awake nights! For the love of God, Shakespeare, what does the flavor *matter?*"

"My concern should at least prove to you," Leonidas returned, "that I believe sufficiently in your quart of ice cream to wish to ascribe a flavor to it. I also believe every word of your apple-munching monkey, and your mink coat. Er—simple, straightforward items, all of them. A nice change, as my good friend Mrs. Mullet would say, from ordinary, common garden clews. What did you do after discovering that your little miscellany had vanished into thin air?"

"I went outside and got into the car and drove away. But I couldn't bring myself to stay away—I can't explain it!" Shaver made a little gesture of helplessness. "The whole thing haunted me! I couldn't stay away, and I didn't want to return. Finally I parked the car on that back street by the garden gate—Ivanhoe Road, I think it's named—and walked through the garden to the house, and wandered around the place, as I told you. I wanted to know what was going on, and I felt that what I'd seen in the hall was somehow important and ought to be told someone, but I didn't want to get mixed up in things my-self. I was in a state of—oh, I don't know how to describe it!"

Leonidas suggested that confusion was a good, com-prehensive word.

"If you can think of something that means confused and stunned and frightened and horrified and generally fouled up, I'd like it better," Shaver said. "Well, I saw you come. And then a little later, that short job with the sour puss and the Hitler mustache. But no woman. Lucky I parked where I did—I'm sure no one spotted the car or the license plate. Now, sir, what about your part in Operation Balderston?"

"Because I should very much like to start making cer-tain inquiries as soon as possible," Leonidas said, "I'll be as succinct as I can. But it seems only fair to suggest that you settle yourself comfortably!"

Omitting all the preliminary details which involved his projected Haseltine manuscript, he began his recital at the point where he had turned back from his front door to get the brown paper-wrapped bank report from his study, only to find that it had been stolen.

"Bank report?" Shaver interrupted. "You mean that investment report? Oh, I've seen that! I ran off three dozen copies on the mimeograph yesterday morning. Why would anyone want to steal that thing? It's just about as secret and important as a classified ad—Shakespeare, look! It's *snow*ing!"

Leonidas put on his pince-nez and gazed out at the flat, drab Carnavon landscape.

"It has absolutely no business snowing!" he said with a touch of severity. "It's only November—and we have problems enough without it! I cannot imagine why the old octopus of fate should stretch out its tentacles in any such hostile exercise!"

"You must know Haseltine to bring up the old octopus of fate!" Shaver said with a laugh. "*Ah, vieux octopus du destin!* I read *le lieutenant galant* every step of the way from St. Lo to Berlin. In French!"

"Indeed?"

"Yes, we set up a command post in what was left of a French library, and the only whole books were all translations of Haseltine. My outfit went for 'em the way they'd have gone after Mom's chocolate cake. Just a breath of home! You know, I thought of *le galant* when I saw Uncle Fenwick. *Le galant* never would have bolted from the scene the way I did!"

"Er—faced with reality," Leonidas said, "who knows? But to continue my story—"

When he finished, Shaver leaned back against the seat and laughed until he started to choke and cry at the same time.

"No wonder my disappearing monkey and the quart of ice cream and the mink coat all seemed perfectly natural

77

to you! Well, you still have your little brown paper package—and what about this green pocketbook? Let's take a look at the thing!"

Leonidas put out a restraining hand as Shaver reached to switch on the dome light of the car.

"I wonder," he said, "if perhaps from now on it will not be wiser to—er—illuminate ourselves as little as possible? While I wish to examine that purse—"

"Illuminate ourselves? But no one saw you!" Shaver said. "No one saw *me!* No one saw the car—and besides, we're *out* of Dalton! We're in Carnavon!"

"M'yes. But I'm quite sure that by now the police of Dalton have thoroughly discussed the Balderston affair with all their many friends in the many surrounding towns. However one may feel about the way in which their minds do or do not work, one must admit that their communications are excellent!"

"But—we weren't seen!"

"Thor and Inga know very well what I look like—and I shouldn't be too sanguine, if I were you, either about myself or about the car."

"I'm *sure* no one saw the car!" Shaver persisted.

"If Fenwick's neighbors are at all like mine," Leonidas said, "some small boy can and will give the police an exact description, including the model type, and the bore and stroke of the piston. And some passerby who hasn't used Ivanhoe Road in years will rush wildly to the police station to gasp out the license plate number and tell how by the strangest coincidence, he or she went via Ivanhoe Road this evening!"

"Shakespeare, you depress me! What're we going to do? After all, we can't just *sit* here while the snow mounts

78

around us—because this isn't any little flurry! This is going to be a real, honest-to-God storm!"

"I think that the most important thing at the moment," Leonidas said as he rubbed his hands together in an effort to restore their circulation, "is some hot food. And some hot coffee. Aren't there any number of roadside restaurants up ahead somewhere?"

"Look, it doesn't add up, Shakespeare!" Shaver protested. "If you think the cops are already so hot on our trail that we don't even dare turn on a dome light, how can we go dropping casually into Mike's Hamburg Palace for a snack? I mean, is because it's after nine and we're both virtually starving *enough?*"

"I'm sure that the police will not expect their supposed murderer and his supposed accomplice—or however they may choose to label you—to drop into Mike's for a plate of hamburgs-with," Leonidas said. "But they will unquestionably notice a lighted, parked car—they always do. And their eyes will also be peeled for speeders who have an aura of desperate flight about them. It was not my intention to alarm you into an unduly defeatist attitude, Shaver. I merely felt that you should be on guard. Er—you haven't several good warm ulsters secreted about this vehicle of yours, by some happy chance?" Leonidas turned up his collar and blew on his fingers.

"Don't I wish I did! But let me tell you that when I left my little room at Mrs. Beming's boarding house this evening, I was in such a lather about this bank examiner business that I didn't need a coat, or think of taking one! When you start in your first job at twenty-six, you don't take things as lightly as you would if you were *young*, you know!"

"Oh, indeed not!" Leonidas agreed gravely. "By no means! Five years in the service, I gather?"

"Yes, and then I finished up college—I ran into Uncle Fenwick in the club after a game in September," Shaver added absently. "We got to talking, and he offered me this opening. After all, when you start your career practically in your dotage, you might as well start with something solid, like a bank. Let's see, I *used* to keep an old trench coat in the rear hatch—no, damn it, there's nothing in there now but Joe Gallup's old violin that I forgot to take back to him!"

"Er—will you get it out, please?" Leonidas said briskly.

"Get it *out*? Oh, I see! You want a fiddle ready for the burning of Rome, or Carnavon, or something?"

"And while you're getting it," Leonidas went on blandly, "do please remember to smear your license plate with snow, or mud, or any handy obliterating substance, won't you?"

Shaver looked at him and shook his head, but he got the violin.

"I suppose," he said as he dumped the case on Leonidas's lap, "they didn't call you The Brain for nothing—that is, I *hope* they didn't! Look, I'm as starved and cold as you are, but d'you really think we ought to take the chance of going to any of these eateries?"

"Why not? Particularly," Leonidas said, "if you have a pair of sun glasses."

"In the glove place in front of you—look, you're not feeling faint, are you, Shakespeare? I mean, I don't know how symptoms of frostbite and the madness of exposure creep on—"

"I'm quite sane," Leonidas assured him. "Er—shall we

start? Because with a violin and dark glasses, you see, I become a kindly old bearded musician. I have nothing in common with that murderous creature with the beard for whom the Dalton police and their friends are doubtless industriously searching."

"And what," Shaver asked as he started up the car, "what does that make me, dear Music Master?"

"You can be a piano player, or a virtuoso on the slap-bass—anything you choose, in fact, which the union saves you from carrying."

"I keep thinking of McLean, and Fell, and that pocketbook—Bill Shakespeare, this road is good and greasy already! See us weave?—and all the other things we ought to be looking into," Shaver said. "I ask myself if we shouldn't be getting to them instead of pausing to stuff ourselves with food. Take *le lieutenant galant*—you wouldn't catch him being a slave to his stomach!"

"If Haseltine doesn't stop to refresh himself occasionally, he certainly should," and certainly would, Leonidas thought privately. "Isn't that a restaurant ahead, with all those lights?"

"It's a Devlin's Thirty-one Flavors—and it's too crowded, Bill. I don't like it!"

"Wait." Leonidas peered through the snow-covered windshield. "Hm. A bus disgorging its passengers—let's stop, Shaver, and mingle with them. We'll be less conspicuous in a group."

At the crowded entrance, the blare of a radio rose above the blare of the juke box.

"Brutal murder of Dalton's most distinguished citizen," an announcer was saying. "The murderer escaped with his accomplice, and all police are hereby requested to keep a sharp lookout for a coupé bearing Massachusetts license plate number 68807. Have *you* used Frigid's Frozen Foods? Frigid's Frozen Foods save you many hours of back-breaking, old-fashioned kitchen toil! Frigid's Frozen Foods save your hands, keep you always lovely, always young, always fresh! *Try* Frigid's Frozen Foods tonight and prove to yourself that Frigid's Frozen Food products, spelled F-r-i-g-i-d—"

7

SHAVER STARTED to push his way out again, but Leonidas took a firm grip on his arm.

"Shakespeare, we *can't*—"

"We can't perch in doorways, trembling like leaves, and we've got to thaw out! If you will recall your Haseltine," Leonidas led him to a corner table, "the gallant lieutenant never hesitates! Sit down!"

"Well," Shaver said, "well, it's so damned full of smoke in here, I can hardly make out your face, so I suppose it's all right if they've described you—or me! Nobody could recognize us! You know, you *look* like a pitiful musician —sort of wan and hungry and cold!"

"In your raffish, uncombed, and slightly blotched condition," Leonidas returned as he laid the violin case conspicuously on the table, "you rather resemble a third-rate night club piano player. Coffee, please," he told the hovering waitress with a smile, "and six hamburgs. Yes, with, please. And rare."

"Double it," Shaver said.

"And now, I want to show you the little present I bought my niece for her birthday."

Leonidas put the green leather pocketbook on the table between them, and unfastened the chromium beetle that served as a clasp.

He might just as well have been telling the truth, he thought regretfully, instead of inventing something for the waitress to overhear as she stood nearby, writing down their order.

For the pocketbook was nearly bare enough to *be* brand new!

Instead of the usual feminine jumble of cigarettes, powder, hairpins, wallets, cash purses, key chains, address books, matches, lighters, pencils, lists, Kleenex, aspirin, and assorted snapshots, this bag contained only a lipstick, a comb, and forty cents in dimes.

"Whoever she is, she's abnormal!" Shaver said promptly.

Leonidas agreed. "She's incredible! Never before in my life did I ever view such a—a sparse, such an impersonal little accumulation! All it tells us is that she has hair which she combs, lips which she lipsticks, and that she budgets herself to four dimes! Well, Shaver, she can certainly have no connection whatsoever with your monkey, or your ice cream, or your mink coat—more's the pity, I might add!"

"I'm disappointed," Shaver said, and sounded it. "I don't know why, but I somehow expected we'd find a name and address, and have it turn out to be some gilded girl friend of Uncle Fenwick's who'd killed him in a rage at being jilted, or something like that."

Leonidas stared at him.

"Now why do you feel that Fenwick might have been addicted to gilded girl friends? Mind you," he said, "I'm not insinuating that it was beyond his—shall we say, his capabilities? But somehow I always thought of him as a pillar of—hm. I don't know that I ever went so far as to qualify the type of pillar, but I definitely placed him in the pillar group."

"According to my father," Shaver said with a chuckle, "Fenwick's college youth was strictly on the rakish side. Stanley Steamers, chorus girls, champagne—for all I know, he may have combined the three and drunk champagne from the girls' slippers as they steamed madly through the night. Oh, Uncle Fenwick was a *one!* And when we lived in Dalton, years and years ago, there was always gossip buzzing around about Uncle Fenwick and some little milliner in Pomfret, or some little milliner in Framfield! Of course, Uncle Fenwick always sort of harped on the memory of his Dear Marcia—"

"Dear *who?*" Leonidas interrupted.

"His wife—she died long before I was born. I remember a lot of talk—funny how you absorb things when you're little, and never realize what people mean until years later, isn't it? I remember his talking so solemnly about his sweet memories of Dear Marcia—and then after he'd gone, mother would let out with a lot of acid cracks about all Fenwick's little milliners. It used to puzzle me," Shaver said. "I kept wondering why Uncle Fenwick couldn't get his hats at Mr. Winston's Haberdashery, like father. No, Bill Shakespeare, Uncle Fenwick was not one hundred percent pillar!"

"And yet," Leonidas said, "that mink coat hardly suggests any little milliner around the corner!"

"To me," Shaver retorted, "it suggests a smart little milliner with a rich, pillar-y friend—don't underestimate Uncle Fenwick! He wasn't a poor lad struggling to get along. He was with dough. And not bad-looking—people were always mistaking him for a governor, or a senator!"

"M'yes, quite. But I should think that perhaps at his age—"

"Age? What's *age* got to do with it? Your redheaded waitress—"

"*What* redheaded waitress?" Leonidas interrupted.

"Well, *ours*, then, chum! Now don't tell me you didn't notice that redheaded job!"

"I didn't," Leonidas told him honestly. "When I came in, my pince-nez were too steamed—"

"Oh? You just smiled at her that way on general principles, did you? Don't kid your old friend Shaver! That little ball of fire's been giving you the well-known eye since we came in—and don't look so bothered and embarrassed, Shakespeare! Those three sailors at the counter are asking themselves bitterly what you've got that they don't seem to have—"

He broke off as the redheaded waitress came back with their order.

"Gee," she said, smiling down at Leonidas as she moved the green pocketbook aside, "gee, that's *keen!* I bet your niece'll go for *that*, all right! *Any* girl would! Everything all right, huh?" she added. "Got enough mustard? Enough relish? Want any more catsup? More cream?"

"Everything's splendid, thank you," Leonidas told her politely.

Privately he decided that if the new Haseltine offered any opportunity for the insertion of a good gutty girl character, this redhead was the exact answer to what she should look like. Small, pert, blue-eyed, lithe, lissom, lush, luscious—he heard Shaver's subdued, insinuating chuckle, and abruptly turned his attention from the girl to his hamburgs. Neither Shaver nor anyone else, including the sailors across the way, would ever believe that his impersonal scrutiny was purely in the interests of his profession!

"Er—splendid! Thank you," he said again, when she gave no indication of going away.

"Want dessert?"

"Thank you, no," Leonidas said. "I fear we haven't time. Perhaps we could have the check? Thank you—er—thank you so much!"

"See what I mean about age?" Shaver said, turning his head to watch the girl as she departed. "Did *I* get any of Toots's time? Come to think of it, *le lieutenant galant* has that same devastating charm. Girls always hover over him, bursting with—"

"Nothing but maternal instinct!" Leonidas interrupted with firmness.

"What a terribly re*fin*ed way of putting it! No one ever tries to—to *mother* me! Must be my glasses—oh, *you* wear them too, don't you? Now I wonder why—"

"I wish," Leonidas tried not to hear a bus driver's long low whistle as he passed by the redhead, "I wish, since you brought up this milliner angle, that you would offer some constructive suggestions!"

"I told you, I knew Uncle Fenwick best when I was roughly twelve! But there's his secretary—"

"Secretary?" Leonidas shook his head as he thought of Miss Scaife, with her Charles Dana Gibson pompadour, and her high voice which bit off words so carefully, and her glasses whose thin gold chain kept popping back into a large gold pin on her bony shoulder. "And that high-necked shirtwaist, and those papers she keeps wrapped around her wrists, and—oh, I don't think I should seriously consider Miss Scaife!"

"Who said anything about the witching Scaife—and I do mean witch! She retired as of last week—she's marrying the principal of the high school. We all kicked in five bucks apiece and gave her a handsome silver-plated jam pot, or something—d'you know this food is doing me a world of good? I feel almost pre-bank examiner," Shaver said cheerfully. "And Uncle Fenwick made a lovely speech about duty and service and loyalty, and gave her a handsome check. You wouldn't have known the old bank, we were that gay and festive. Cider in paper cups, and a white cake with 'BEST WISHES' squidged all over it in pink frosting, and Auld Lang Syne off key. You sure you don't want some dessert? I mean, in a nutshell, the *new* secretary."

"And what is she like?" Leonidas asked curiously. "Er —more Scaife?"

"She's a honey, Bill Shakespeare. Strictly a Powers model girl. A Miss Cowe—with an 'e,'" he added. "Not like cow, the animal. A blonde thing. In green—that is, she wore green today, her first day. A neat green tweed suit, magnificently draped about a magnificent form, with—"

"Green?" Leonidas said, and tried to recall Mrs. Mullet's comments about the blonde girl who had brought the bank report to his house. "Green?"

"Yes, green—I'm on to you, Bill. You're just picking up the color to prove your complete lack of personal interest. Faker!"

"On the contrariwise," Leonidas said, "I'm attempting to identify her as the girl who brought that report to my house. Blonde, Mrs. Mullet said. Green tweed, round silver buttons, glasses—what *does* one call those weirdly shaped things? Pixies?"

"I just call 'em crazy. But that's our Miss Cowe, crazy glasses and all. Doubtless by now, *you'd* be calling her Baby, or even by her first name, whatever it is. But me, Mrs. Shaver's little boy, our Miss Cowe mistook for some escaped leper. I even had to pry the Cowe name out of our Mr. McLean—by the way, how's for looking into him, now? He lives here in Carnavon." Shaver crumpled up an empty cigarette package. "But before we lay any plans, I'm going to fight my way through the pinballs to the cigarette machine—be right back."

Leonidas nodded, and put the green pocketbook down on the bench beside him.

Idly, he picked up the little brown paper package and looked at it casually.

As he surveyed the label, he could feel the hairs standing up straight on the back of his neck.

Taking off his pince-nez, he carefully polished them, avoiding the while the interested gaze of the redhead, who was watching him from a few feet away.

He wanted no optical errors about the name and address on that label.

But there it was, in black and white!

> Mrs. Yeoville Pushing
> 5 Birch Hill Road
> Dalton Centre 81 Mass.

The fact that he had snatched a package which was not his from that woman with the stovepipe hat, Leonidas thought, took some digesting.

But it accounted for a lot. It at least explained her prompt, indignant reaction.

And whether the package belonged to Emily Pushing, and the woman was taking it to her, or whether it was something which Emily had given the woman, wrapped up in that paper, was all beside the point.

What it didn't account for was—who had taken his bank report, and where was it?

Basically, he was right back where he had started!

He looked up from his study of the label just in time to see Yeoville Pushing, with Emily by his side, coming in the doorway.

There was no optical error about them, either!

They hadn't seen him yet, but they would as soon as they finished brushing the snow from their shoulders. Yeoville and Emily always saw everyone, everywhere. They made a point of it. Seeing people they knew was virtually their life work.

And the Pushing radio was never still. They would have been the first to have heard about Fenwick. They would certainly know about *him!*

And what they might know about that brown paper package, which Emily would most assuredly spot at once!

His muttered exclamation, more audible than he had intended it to be, brought the redhead to his side in a flash.

"What's the matter?" she leaned over him, blocking his view of the door. "Oh—somebody come in you don't want to see, huh?"

"Yes." Leonidas managed a weak smile as he withdrew some bills from his wallet and laid them on the check. "Is there, by some chance, a rear entrance?"

"Sure—gee, thanks! Sure, I'll show you. Come along."

Grabbing up the green pocketbook, the brown paper package, and the violin case, Leonidas followed her as she wove expertly around tables and through alcoves to the rear of the restaurant. He ignored the ribald comments of the sailors at the counter, and more long low whistles from an admiring truck driver.

"Fresh!" the redhead said. "*Fresh!* Here you are—it's the emergency door, right behind that trellis thing, like. Don't pay any mind to all the cops outside. They—"

"Er—*cops?*"

"Yeah. They're just Dalton cops. They're waiting to pick up a couple guys when they go to get into a coupé parked out there, that's all."

8

"OH," LEONIDAS SAID. "Oh, indeed!"

"Of course, they hadn't ought to be over here," she went on lightly, "but there's this Carnavon cop, Bill MacCobble, that's got a brother that's a Dalton cop, and so—what's the matter? Aren't you going out?"

"Under the circumstances," Leonidas said, "er—no! I've changed my mind."

"Oooh! Oooh!" The sparkling blue eyes that looked up at him grew suddenly serious. "*Ooop!* You mean—*you— you—?*"

"M'yes," Leonidas said. "Quite so. It was my intention to whip out to that very coupé, but I'm sure you'll agree with me that it's hardly a very wise course at the moment."

"Gee, Mr. Witherall, you're in a *spot*—oh, sure, *I* know who you are! This is but definitely not good! Because I heard a cop say that if those two guys didn't come out pretty soon, they'd come *in!* And they most probably will!"

With a touch of resignation, Leonidas agreed that they most probably would.

"Say—I got an idea, Mr. Witherall! There's only one place you'll be safe, even though you probably won't like it much—you come along with me!"

She ducked into a short passageway, pulling him after

her into the kitchen. With a series of forceful tugs, she jerked him out of the path of waitresses with laden trays, kept him from colliding with bus boys bearing stacks of dishes and glasses, and saved him from being annihilated by a perspiring cook who was juggling a mammoth steel wash boiler whose contents bubbled ominously.

Leonidas noticed with interest that all the faces wore a universal expression of dreamy blankness very similar to the preoccupied stare of Meredith boys during examinations.

And while everybody was shouting wildly at everybody else, no one seemed to be answering, or even expecting an answer.

"Here," the redhead gave his arm another firm tug. "*This* way—"

Leaving the kitchen through a swinging door, they arrived at another narrow passageway.

"Here!" she said in triumph, and pointed. "Here we are!"

"*There?*" Leonidas looked up at the chaste little neon sign that said "Ladies Lounge."

"Sure! You'll be *safe* in there, Mr. Witherall! Come—"

"I can't!" Leonidas told her flatly. "I absolutely balk! My dear child—"

"Listen, Mr. Witherall, you *got* to! Come *on*—oh, first I better make sure the coast's clear—"

She darted into the lounge, then darted out, grabbed him, and jerked him inside the small, square pink room whose wealth of chromium-framed mirrors reflected Leonidas accusingly back at himself into infinity.

"Get in here!" She pulled open a mirrored door and

disclosed a shallow closet filled with brooms, mops, and dirty towels. "Come on—wedge yourself in somehow—and but very quick!"

"I cannot—"

"Mr. Witherall, you get *in!*"

When he still hung back, she put both hands against his chest and shoved him in, herself.

"There!" she said. "You'll be perfectly safe, honest you will. I'll just lock you in here and take the key with me—only for my sake, don't you make any sounds, see? Not a peep!"

"But—"

"I'll be back soon as those cops clear out—I'm off in a few minutes anyway, at ten, and I'll take care of you. You'll be okay. Don't worry—"

"But look here—" Leonidas protested as she started to close the closet door.

"Look here yourself, Mr. Witherall!" she retorted. "It's either you hide in the sandbox here, or else you make like a clam and go jump into the kitchen fat kettle, and that's all there is about it!"

"I'm resigned," Leonidas told her gently, "to the—er—sandbox. It's my friend—d'you think you could manage to warn that young man who was with me?"

"Gee!" she said blankly. "I know there *was* someone, but gee, I don't know what he looked like! I never noticed him!"

"Tall, thin, young, glasses—"

"Someone's *coming!*"

The closet door was shut, and Leonidas heard the key turn in the lock.

The old octopus of fate was in one of its more whimsical moods, he decided, for the newcomer who entered the pink lounge as the redheaded waitress left was none other than Emily Pushing.

He knew beyond any doubt that it was Emily, because she was singing the same solo which she had sung at church the previous Sunday—and she was flatting the same notes.

She was followed by two girls whose dates were not beginning to live up to expectations, one woman with a slight crying jag, and a quartet of outspoken females whose biologic commentaries would have thrown Haseltine's Lady Alicia into a state of shocked coma.

If that fifteen-minute dash earlier in the evening around Birch Hill Road had seemed like hours, this interlude was several eternities in comparison.

The really trying aspect of the situation, he thought, would be his utter inability to utilize his gleanings conversationally, at some later date. While it was always a simple matter to begin some dissertation with a casual "As I overheard several women saying on the bus, the other day," neither his Birch Hill neighbors nor his Meredith colleagues nor even the understanding and sympathetic Mrs. Mullet would conceivably understand a preface which described his present status. "As I overheard several women in the—" Leonidas shook his head. He couldn't do it. No one could.

And no matter how hard he tried, he found himself quite unable to devote his full attention to the problems of Fenwick Balderston's murder, which certainly *should* be sufficiently distracting!

After a while, he gave up trying. He didn't even attempt to figure out who this redheaded child could be who had befriended him so magnanimously.

But he drew a long breath of relief at the gay, pert whistle which announced her return.

"Okay, chum!" her voice said cheerfully. "Just wait a bit till a few of the girls scram out of the hall outside."

"Did they get my friend?" Leonidas asked in a whisper. "Did the police get Shaver?"

"No, they didn't get anybody. He must've beat it. They looked all through the place, and then they left one guy out by the coupé, and went away—hey, there's fourteen inches of snow already, and it's still snowing! They say three feet before—ooop! Company coming!"

When she finally led him out into the hall some ten minutes later, she looked at him curiously.

"Were there many of 'em like those two?" she inquired briefly.

"Er—yes," Leonidas said. "M'yes. Yes, indeed!"

"I thought so! You don't look shattered, even. Gee, most of the men *I* know would've died at what those two were saying! In my candied opinion, Mr. Witherall, you're an old sport, that's what! Come on, sneak out this back door, quick, before anybody sees you!"

"In my candied opinion," Leonidas felt tears come to his eyes as the first cold blast of north wind and snow struck his face, "in my candied opinion, you're some relation of Mrs. Mullet's!"

"Sure—gee, didn't you recognize me? I thought she probably told you all about me—she told *me* all about *you!* I knew you right away! I'm her niece that's just come to live with her—where's that big lug? He said he'd be right here! I mean my boy friend," she added in explanation. "He's supposed to be waiting here for us!"

"You're Daphne!" Leonidas said, making terrific demands on his memory.

"That's my sister. *I'm* Chloe."

"Indeed! Er—are you ever referred to as Amber, I wonder?"

"Most usually, everybody just always calls me Red—there he is, and about time!" she said as a dilapidated sedan churned through the snow and came to a stop in front of them. "Get in front, Mr. Witherall. There's plenty room for the three of us. Meet my friend Kilroy—hi, Kilroy, meet Mr. Witherall."

Kilroy, an enormous youth in a very light, very fitted polo coat with heavily padded shoulders and a belt that tied, jumped out from behind the wheel and helped stuff them into the car.

"I'm pleased to meet your acquaintance, Mr. Witherall," he said politely, and then added in more informal tones, "Say, pal, ain't you got a coat? You'll freeze like that!"

"Give him yours, Kilroy," Red said. "You got a spare jacket on the back seat!"

"Okay, sugar. Here, pal, get out and put this on!"

"My dear Kilroy, I couldn't dream of depriving you of your—"

"You get right out of the car and slip it on, Mr. Witherall!" Red said firmly. "Auntie wouldn't ever forgive me if I let you catch cold. Auntie works for Mr. Witherall, Kilroy. He's a *writer!*"

"Is that right?" Kilroy bundled Leonidas into the polo coat, and then donned a short leather jacket with a lambskin collar. "I never seen a real writer before," he went on as he climbed back into the car. "But you sure *look* like one, pal. Play the fiddle, too?"

"Er—no. It belongs to a friend. You don't mind if I put it and this other truckle," Leonidas indicated the brown paper package and the green pocketbook, "in the back, I hope?"

The polo coat fitted him rather like an oversized bathrobe, but he felt like purring like a kitten at its warmth. He stuffed his hands in the pockets.

"All in?" Kilroy asked. "Squeeze yourself out of my way, sugar, I can't get to the gear shift. Where we going?"

"Where *are* we going, Mr. Witherall?" Red asked him.

"From the looks of the elements," Leonidas said, "I rather wonder if we're going anywhere!"

"This old bus of mine," Kilroy spoke of it fondly, as if it were an old and trusted friend, "can go anywheres you want to go. Say, what do you know? A fellow was telling me they can't do any ploughing because the snow ploughs are all in the storage shed, see, and they can't get through to the storage shed without they have ploughs to plough the way, see? What a joke on the street department boys, huh?"

"Maybe it'll teach 'em a lesson," Red said. "They ought to know better. Where do you want to go, Mr. Witherall? Now don't be polite—you must want to go somewheres! You know, the cops are after Mr. Witherall, Kilroy," she added as an afterthought.

"Is that right! What for, hey?"

"They think I murdered a man in Dalton," Leonidas

said, "and it seems only fair to suggest that the conse-
quences might be most unpleasant for you and Red if I
am found in your company."

"What he means," Red translated for Kilroy's benefit,
"is you hadn't ought to let us get picked up by any
cops. Not for anything! The big dopes, to think that *you'd*
kill anyone!"

"I'll see to the cops. Say, pal, *did* you?" Kilroy seemed
to take a more realistic attitude concerning murder, Leonidas thought, than did Red.

"Er—no!"

"My brother knew a man got pinched for murder. He
didn't do it, but he got twenty years all the same," Kilroy
said. "And then my uncle knew another man killed this
guy he found with his wife, and the cops never touched
him. Never found him. It's just as it turns out, I always
say. You want to go somewheres in Dalton, or Carnavon,
or where? In this type weather, it's better if you keep
moving."

"Actually," Leonidas said, "I should like to go to the
home of a man named Fergus McLean, somewhere in
Carnavon. I don't know the address."

"We'll stop at the drugstore and you can look it up in
the phone book," Red said as the car started to churn its
way out of the restaurant's parking space. "I don't know,
though—the Frigid's Frozen Foods news man said something about your beard, Mr. Witherall, so maybe I better
go in. You can write the name down for me."

Although to Leonidas the highway seemed strewn with
snow-crusted cars whose owners had abandoned them to
the storm, the dilapidated sedan churned on steadily into
the center of Carnavon.

Kilroy pulled up in front of a drugstore, and Red, clutching a paper bearing McLean's name, went inside.

"That's the police station, see, right over there," Kilroy pointed it out earnestly, as if he felt it were a beauty spot Leonidas shouldn't be permitted to miss. "Say, Mr. Witherall, I keep thinking I seen you somewheres before. You in the army, hey?"

"Not this war."

"I'm sure I seen you. I never forget faces. Say, you know what?"

"Er—what?" Leonidas asked obediently.

"Well, it's something I thought about a lot when I was in the army. Kind of a dream, like. I never told Red, but I can tell you because you're a writer, see, and you'd understand—" Kilroy paused.

"D'you want to write a book?" Leonidas knew from experience that was what people usually had in mind after such a preamble.

"Write a *book?*" Kilroy stared at him in horror. "My God, no! I never—oh, here she comes back. Got it, sugar?"

"Florence Street. Number Twenty-four. That's between Hazel Road and Grace Avenue—say, Mr. Witherall, the radio was on in there. They want you, but bad! And they said progress was being made in the search for you, and they had you under sur—sur—"

"Surveillance?" Leonidas suggested.

"That's it! Do you think so, or do you think they're just *say*ing that?"

Leonidas smiled as he watched a police car pull away from the snow-banked curb in front of the Carnavon police station.

"I rather suspect," he said, "that they're just saying it.

Otherwise that prowl car would have swooped over here, don't you think, and arrested us where, so to speak, we sat?"

Red hooked his arm in hers, and hugged it excitedly to her.

"Gee," she said, "it's thrilling! Won't Auntie be sore when she hears how she missed this!"

It was, Leonidas thought as the sedan churned its steady way past still more abandoned cars, one way of considering the situation.

Number Twenty-four Florence Street, a small, old-fashioned frame house with a front porch, turned out to be brilliantly lighted from attic to cellar. Throngs of people seemed to be moving about inside, and the general gaiety was audible even over the chugging of Kilroy's motor.

"Gee!" Red said. "A party!"

"Looks like a *good* party!" Kilroy added. "We going, pal?"

Leonidas reflected for a moment.

"M'yes, I think you two are—briefly. Ring the bell, Red, pretend that you want Twenty-four Grace—or Mabel or Hazel or Maude Street— and that you've got your streets twisted in the storm because the snow has obliterated the signs. See if you can find out what this party is about."

"You mean, 'Gee, it *sounds* like such a lovely party! Somebody's birthday, I bet?'"

"Exactly. Then come back and let me know—and what about your feet? You'll get soaked in those drifts along the front walk!"

"*I* know what! I'll carry her," Kilroy said with relish. "Come on, sugar! Let's go!"

101

While it was impossible to think that there might be a home in the land into which Mr. Frigid had not poured his frosted news by now, and impossible to think that Fergus McLean had not heard about Fenwick's murder, Leonidas found it equally impossible to believe that Mc-Lean would be throwing a party of these proportions if he *did* know about it.

Kilroy, still happily bearing Red in his arms, came wading back through the snow to the car.

"Here, pal!"

Leonidas stared in some amazement at the handful of cigars which Kilroy was thrusting out at him over Red's shoulder.

"Er—thank you so much," he said politely, "but—er— *why?*"

"McLean had triplets today," Red explained. "You get a cigar apiece."

"*What?*"

"Fergus, Angus, and he thinks maybe Campbell." Red giggled as she got into the car. "McLean thinks that's pretty good for a man of fifty-five. He wants we should come back and bring our friends, and any friends of our friends, because any friends of ours are friends of his. He's higher than a kite."

Leonidas began to laugh.

"I must explain to my friend Shaver," he said, "about the fallacy of '*Post hoc, ergo propter hoc.*' Not the bank examiner, in short, caused McLean's jitters this afternoon! And of course everyone at the bank was quietly polite and noncommittal and deadpan—hoping wistfully, no doubt, for the best! Is he really—er—high?"

"But soaring!" Red assured him.

"And that music I heard when the door was open—isn't that a radio?"

"It's a phonograph," Kilroy said. "I could see a bunch gathered around it with a stack of records. Say, pal, why not let's us go in for a quick one, hey? It's a cold, cruel night!"

"Er—let's us indeed!" Leonidas said. "You may pick up your quick one while I ask the excellent McLean several brief questions in a conversational sort of way."

The sight of Leonidas standing on the doorstep brought a flood of happy tears streaming down McLean's cheeks.

"On a night like this, a night like *this*, Mr. Witherall, *you* should come to felici—" He paused. "Come in, come in, come in—Bobby, get Mr. Witherall and his good friends something to warm themselves with! Get cigars, get the young lady a chair—take their coats! That you should come through this dreadful storm to felici—" He paused again. "Oh, Mr. Witherall, I'm as pleased as a little child at the honor you do me! Your felici—uh—your coming means more to me than all the felici—oh, my, oh, my!"

McLean broke down entirely.

"My felicitations," Leonidas assured him, "are heartfelt and—er—ineffable. I'm only so sorry that Shaver, who started out with me, was unable because of—of transportation problems to present his felicitations to you in person."

"Ah, Shaver!" McLean said affectionately. "So *he* was coming to felici—so he was coming, too? Ah, a splendid boy, a fine lad, doing us all great credit, great credit! A chip off the old bock—his father was president of Boston Thrift and Provident for many years before his death, you know! A chip off the old bock—and how did the lad take the news of Mr. Fenwick?"

Leonidas suddenly felt as if a cold wet towel had been slapped smartly across his face.

"Er—the news?" He stalled for time. "News?"

"Ah, modest lad that he is, he never told you about his promotion? He's to be Mr. Fenwick's personal assistant— he was to learn about it tonight at dinner from Mr. Fenwick himself! A fine lad, a fine family, a fine, fine day for him, a milestone, a milestone! A millstone—I mean, a *mile*stone—for me, too, Mr. Witherall, but a hard, hard day! A great, great strain. Let me tell you," he took Leonidas's arm and leaned on it heavily, "let me tell you, Mr. Witherall—"

His somewhat detailed account of the rigors of the day was finally interrupted by the pealing of the doorbell.

Red broke her way expertly through the solid wall of admiring males surrounding her, and walked over to where Leonidas was standing.

"I guess *you* got saved by the bell, all right!" she observed. "That guy's wound up! Say, we going to stay, or had I better start collecting the boy friend? I don't think we should ought to let him play *too* much with that pink brew in the punch bowl, Mr. Witherall—tastes to me like it was laced with dynamite!"

After a quick glance at Kilroy, who had a glass planted in either hand, Leonidas advised her to start collecting forthwith.

They took their leave over McLean's tearful protests and the furious opposition of every man at the party. But the women present, Leonidas noticed, seemed to feel no very deep pain at Red's departure.

"Well," Kilroy said after they had waded through the snow back to the car, "what now, pal?"

Before Leonidas could answer, the scream of a siren cut through the storm.

A police car skidded around the corner just ahead of them, lurched—and stopped dead.

9

"THE GOONS," Kilroy said dispassionately. "Well, I got to tow 'em out of trouble and get 'em started, I suppose. We can't never get past 'em if I don't, that's a cinch!"

The ensuing fifteen minutes which he devoted to extricating the Carnavon police from a snowbank gave both Leonidas and Red, who sat quietly in the car, a certain pleasurable satisfaction.

In fact, by the time Kilroy had used the sedan to push the police car to a start that sent it lurching back around the corner, Leonidas and Red were giggling together like a pair of schoolgirls.

"Could you hear that radio of theirs, pal?" Kilroy inquired. "It said a man with a beard was spotted in Framfield, and more men with beards also been reported as seen in Sudbury, Lexington and Concord!"

"Unquestionably," Leonidas said, "they are now beginning to confuse me with Paul Revere. Through every Middlesex village—m'yes, indeed. Kilroy, that was a heroic rescue, for which I regretfully note that you received absolutely no material reward. Er—by the way, have you a first name?"

Kilroy didn't answer.

"He doesn't like it," Red explained. "It's—hey, can I tell him? I know he won't ever use it on you! His whole name is Clarence Percival Smith, Mr. Witherall. They just *call* him Kilroy. They *always* did!"

"And you always *better*, too!" Kilroy said. "Look, pal, what now? Where to?"

Leonidas reflected for a moment.

"What I should *like* to do," he said at last, "is to telephone a friend of mine in Chicago and see if he can give me any clew as to the identity of a doctor who arrived at the home of the murdered man in Dalton long after the murder was committed, but who—I rather suspect—had been thero earlier in the evening."

"You think this doctor done it, hey?" Kilroy asked.

"I think he well might have," Leonidas said. "It's playing a long shot, admittedly, to telephone about him. The doctor may be using an alias, he may not actually have anything whatsoever to do with Chicago, even though he mentioned a Chicago plano. I can not, furthermore, imagine where I might with safety make such a cull at this point. But I wish very much indeed to find out all that I possibly can about the man."

"Where is he now?" Red demanded.

Leonidas shrugged.

"Who knows? I don't know whether or not he had any luggage with him. I noticed none in Fenwick's front hall. He vouchsafed no information which could lead me to believe that he might be staying either at Balderston Hall as a guest, or even in Dalton itself. On the other hand, since it was he who summoned the police and informed them of the murder, I wonder—m'yes, I wonder if the police might not perhaps desire his presence at least for a brief period?"

"What I mean is," Red said, "if this guy's around anywheres near here, say within fifty miles or so, why bother phoning to Chicago to find out about him, Mr. Witherall?

Why not just get hold of the guy himself and ask him what you want to know?"

"A sterling, an admirable, and a logical thought," Leonidas said, "but—"

"He a big guy?" Kilroy interrupted.

"Er—no. Short, stocky—possibly in his early or middle forties. You would make two of him, Kilroy, with ease."

"Well, then," Kilroy said, "let's us find him, hey? If the cops only made him stick around until after this snow got going, it's a cinch he wouldn't very likely of tramped way into Boston to spend the night. He most likely just stayed right around in Dalton somewheres. So, let's us hunt him up, hey? After all, pal," he added seriously, "murder ain't a rap you brush off like any fly, see. You hadn't ought to leave any loopholes unturned at all!"

"M'yes, but I still find myself wondering!" Leonidas said. "Provided that we could find him and—er—isolate him—for there's a very good chance that he may be nestling under the wing of the Dalton police, you know! But assuming that we could locate the doctor for a quiet chat, I still wonder if we could persuade him to answer our questions with any degree of accuracy? That's quite a point to consider!"

"Oh, Kilroy can take care of that," Red said simply. "Kilroy spent three years in Army Intelligence, didn't you, Kilroy?"

"Three years and two months," he corrected her with pride. "Me, I probably got more guys to answer more questions accurate than anyone you'll ever know, pal! If this guy's in Dalton, and if you'll just figure out where we can get hold of him, why I'll see he answers you accurate, pal! That's a promise, see?"

"Er—where," Leonidas inquired as the sedan started churning off again, "are you—I mean, are *we*, going?"

"Dalton—where else? By the time we get ourselves ploughed over there, pal, you get the place all figured out where he'll be at. *That* hadn't ought to be too tough for a writer, I shouldn't think! I bet if *I* was a writer, *I* could guess what hotel the guy'd pick!"

"Listen, Mr. Witherall will know all right, see?" There was a touch of reproof in Red's voice. "He knows if this doctor's the kind that would stay at the Dalton House like a cheap salesman, or at the Dalton Inn in a nice room with a bath and refined service and all—gee, there isn't any other place he *could* go, is there? And I shouldn't think he'd hardly stay at that house where there was the murder! Which, Mr. Witherall? The Dalton House, or the Dalton Inn?"

"Er—suppose," Leonidas said, "that we try the Dalton Inn."

"There!" Red said. "I told you, Kilroy, Mr. Witherall would know! Auntie says there's *no*thing he doesn't know!"

Or nothing, Leonidas privately amended, of which he could not take prompt advantage after someone else had kindly thought it out for him.

"Gee," she continued wistfully, "I keep thinking of Auntie, and how she'd *love* being here, going to parties and being chased by cops, and a murder and all! Is she ever going to burn when she hears what she missed! She had an awful interesting job tonight, Mr. Witherall, that she took over to help out a friend—say, honestly, Kilroy, I *got* to ask you! How in hell do you know *where* you're going? *Do* you?"

Leonidas didn't wonder at her question. He had yearned to ask the same thing himself.

For all signs and all markers of every description had been completely obliterated by the snow, and all houses and buildings suddenly looked alike. The minute segment of road visible ahead seemed to have neither any beginning nor any ending, nor any breadth. There were no landmarks. There was only snow, and more snow.

"Say, sugar," Kilroy said patiently, "I lived in these parts all my life except for three years and eight months! Do I need any signs to tell me how I should go from Carnavon to Dalton, hey? Don't be dumb. It ain't like you."

They proceeded to churn along in silence, except for the steady chug of the motor, while the speedometer marked off another two miles.

Leonidas found himself thinking of Shaver and what had become of him. Probably when the assorted police closed in on Devlin's Thirty-one Flavors, he had followed the line of least resistance, marched out with all those bus passengers, and rumbled off into the night with them. Probably Shaver was even now sitting in some bus, stalled in some suburban snowbank, waiting until some street department boys somewhere figured out how to get at their ploughs without a plough to clear the way to them.

But in a small way, Leonidas thought, he had personally made some progress. He had disposed of the bank problems in general, and particularly of any specific bank problem as providing a motive for Fenwick's murder. Shaver's suspicions of shortages and of McLean were unfounded. Shaver had been the other guest at Fenwick's, his promotion had occasioned the invitation.

Now there was Doctor Fell.

He wouldn't even permit himself at this point to think beyond Doctor Fell to Shaver's mad miscellany of the monkey eating the Delicious apple, the ice cream which he kept hoping had been pistachio, the mink coat—

"Mr. Witherall," Red said hesitantly, "I don't want to bother your train of thought, like, but there's something I've been simply *dy*ing to ask you! But *pi*ning!"

"Er—yes?"

"Well, I noticed it back at Devlin's when you first came in the door. You had it tucked underneath your arm."

"Oh, that green pocketbook!" Leonidas remembered that she had admired it.

"No, the little brown paper package."

"M'yes, it's on the back seat with the violin of my friend's friend. Er—what about it?"

"Well," Red said, "well—what's in it?"

Leonidas looked at her quizzically.

"So you share your aunt's zest for knowing the contents of little brown paper packages?"

"Gee, I don't know what you mean about sharing her zest, Mr. Witherall, but I just always burn up with curiosity when I see packages and bundles that're wrapped up! I *yearn*," Red said eagerly, "to know what's *in* them! Now phones I don't care about—the phone can ring and ring, and *I* don't pay any mind. Auntie does. She can't *wait* to find out who's calling. She goes running like a deer—and even if it's a wrong number, she won't let the person on the other end get away till she's found out who they are, and what number they really wanted in the first place. She always—what're we stopping here for, Kilroy? Stuck at last, or lost at last, huh?"

"I hate to say it, sugar," Kilroy shook his head, "but I guess this's about as far as we're going to go without chains!"

"What I am at a complete loss to understand," Leonidas said truthfully, "is how you've managed to get this far without any!"

"It's all in knowing how," Kilroy said. "And I know this old bus—no, pal, don't you bother to get out. You don't need to help. I'm just going to snap on some clips. Won't take a minute."

"Where are we, anyway?" Red asked. "Would you be a one to know?"

"Sure, why not? I wanted to duck the Pomfret hills, sugar, so I took the short cut. We're just on the East Carnavon-Dalton line, near the lake."

He took a flashlight from the glove compartment, got out, and slammed the door. Leonidas and Red lost sight of him almost at once, but they heard sounds which indicated that he was getting the clip chains out of the sedan's rear hatch.

"A package similar to the one you were mentioning," Leonidas said, "also intrigued your excellent aunt this afternoon. She—er—pined for me to open it, then. It is my firm intention to confess to her tomorrow that I should have promptly followed her suggestion and found out exactly what was in it."

"You mean you had that package all this time, and you never opened it *yet?*" Red said in awed tones. "But you could of! I mean, you *can! Any* time! Like now."

"M'yes, I can open that little package on the back seat," Leonidas said, "but it is not the little package I had at home this afternoon. Only a twin."

"I don't get it."

"Actually, neither do I, Red. Except that I had a package, someone stole it, I snatched it from the apparent thief, and discovered back at Thirty-one Flavors that I had instead stolen a package which looked like mine, but bore someone else's name and address. Er—I trust that's quite clear?"

"Not very. But what's in this package you *got?*"

"I have not," Leonidas told her, "had the opportun—"

The car door was suddenly jerked open, and a flashlight was focussed on his face.

"A beard!" A man's voice—and it wasn't Kilroy's—exclaimed in triumph. "A beard! Well, mister, let's—"

"Hey, *you!*" A flashlight was in turn suddenly focussed on the policeman whose light was still causing Leonidas to blink. "Hey, what's the big idea?" Kilroy demanded truculently, as he stabbed his light in the direction of another looming figure. "What you two guys think you're doing, hey?"

"We're—oh, hi, bud!" There was a definite change in the policeman's tone as he recognized Kilroy. "Hi! Say, thanks for helping us out of that snowbank back on Florence Street, bud. We couldn't stop to thank you then, once we got started."

"Don't mention it, pal!" Kilroy said coldly. "Any time, pal! Just scaring the hell out of my uncle in payment, hey, that's all?"

"Your uncle? Oh. You see," the cop sounded a little embarrassed, "you see, we're hunting this man with a beard, see, and so—"

"Yeah? And what're you hunting my uncle for, pal?" Kilroy's voice became even icier. "He's been playing his fiddle over at McLean's party on Florence Street, see, not doing no harm I can think of unless you don't happen to like the type music he plays, maybe?" His flashlight seemed to waver in his hand for a moment, and the beam —as if by the merest accident—pointed out the violin case in the back seat of the sedan. "Like your fiddles hot, hey? Or is playing a fiddle got to be a crime since I been away in the service, maybe? Tell me all about it, pal! Tell me what my uncle done—"

"Listen, bud, don't go getting sore! It's all a mistake. We—"

"It better be, pal!"

"You trying to go to Dalton, bud?" The cop's tones were almost conciliatory now. "Because they tell us the streets over there are even worse than Carnavon. They can't get to the ploughs because they haven't any ploughs to plough their way to the maintenance sheds, see? I don't think you'll be able to make it—"

"Listen, pal, I'm taking my girl friend home," Kilroy said, "and I'm taking my uncle and his fiddle home, and I'm going to make it all right, see—unless you want to make something of it! And how many more of you cops are going to be stopping me and yelling your heads off at my uncle, hey?"

"All right, bud, all right, all right! We'll chat with the Dalton crowd and tell 'em we checked up on you—what's your license number?" The cop fumbled with cold hands for his notebook and pencil.

Kilroy told them, enunciating each syllable of each number with exquisite clarity.

"Okay, bud, we got it! We'll tell Dalton if you manage to get over there, you and your uncle are all okay!"

"*If* he don't get pneumonia with you letting the snow drift all over the poor old—"

The sedan's door was slammed shut, and the rest of the conversation was lost to Leonidas and Red.

She giggled.

"It's just as it turns out, isn't it, as Kilroy always says!"

"M'yes," Leonidas said thoughtfully, "it is. Er—I think it proves something, too. Either that a virtuous and kindly deed is always rewarded, or possibly that at night all cats are black. At this moment, I am admittedly unable to decide which."

"Kilroy's always doing things for people," Red said. "That boy's got a heart big as an ox. Of course sometimes it seems to me like he didn't know more than ten or fifteen words in all, but he's a nice boy—he'd slay me if he heard me say that, too. He likes to think he's the hell of a guy. Gee, I sure wish he could manage to settle himself down, though!" she added with a sigh.

"Er—he's not working?" No mention, Leonidas recalled, had been made of Kilroy's occupation.

"Oh, it isn't that. He never has any trouble getting any job he wants. He's *al*ways working. He's a bodyguard— and it's swell pay. But his heart isn't *in* it! There's something he's wanted to do ever since he came back home, and I can't pry it out of him what it is. I bet *you* could find out, Mr. Witherall—say, would you try if you got the chance?"

"I rather wonder if he didn't start to—m'yes, Red, I'll try," Leonidas said. "It's the very least I can do for you after your infinite kindness in rescuing me—not to mention your utter disregard for your own safety and welfare!"

"Oh, this is fun!" Red said. "I wouldn't've missed this for *any*thing—you know, I had a date with you tomorrow night anyway, Mr. Witherall!"

"Er—indeed?"

"Sure, it's my night off, and I'm going to help Auntie take care of that club meeting of yours—gee, didn't she tell you?"

"While she mentioned a niece, I took it for granted that she referred to your sister Daphne. I think I may safely say, Red, that your presence will do the morale of the Collectors' Club a world of good."

"Auntie told me," she paused and giggled, "well, I suppose I shouldn't tell you this, but she said they were as big a bunch of old bottom-pinchers as she ever laid eye on, but otherwise very educated and refined gentlemen. Honest, Mr. Witherall," she went on rather hurriedly, "don't you *care* what's in that little brown paper package at *all?*"

"Although it is the unquestioned property of Emily Pushing," Leonidas said, "or at least wrapped up in paper bearing her plainly printed name, I wonder if perhaps we have not—m'yes, I think that we've earned the right to inspect its contents. Reach over and get it, please, Red, and let us discover, before anything else befalls us, exactly what it contains."

Kilroy returned from his labors in time to hold the flashlight for the grand opening.

Once the string was untied and the brown paper removed, the trio sat and stared.

"Well, gee!" Red said at last. "Gee, I never was more disappointed! It's a—it's—say, Mr. Witherall, what the hell *is* it, anyway?"

116

"It looks," Leonidas said critically, "like a small, common ordinary piece of grey slate. Er—what's your candied opinion, Red?"

She thought for a moment.

"Well, if it was even instead of being sort of lopsided, and smooth instead of so uneven, and if it had maybe a coat of nice enamel and some decorations of some kind," she said, "why, I'd call it something you maybe would sit a teapot on, or a pot of geraniums, or something. Or else somebody just pinched a piece out of somebody's front flagstone walk."

"Kilroy," Leonidas said, "d'you entertain any constructive thoughts on the identity of this strange object?"

"Rubble," Kilroy said promptly. "It's just a piece of rubble, pal. Some boy brought it home to his folks as a souveneer of London. It's a piece off one of them slate rooves. I seen plenty of 'em when I was there, pal. It ain't nothing else but rubble."

Red re-wrapped the small piece of slate in its brown paper, and carefully re-tied the string. Leonidas returned the package to its place on the back seat.

"I hope if you ever find out what the hell it is, you'll let me know, Mr. Witherall," Red said. "Because I'm going to keep wondering to my dying day! And besides what anyone would want it *for*, why would anyone just *want* it, anyway?"

"I suspect that Kilroy's notion of souvenir rubble is the soundest," Leonidas remarked as the car once again started off. "The only other thing I ever saw which even remotely resembles that object was in a glass case at the Peabody Museum, and its identification tag had succumbed to the ravages of time. While I think it pertained

117

in some obscure way to Cro-Magnon man, it might on the other hand have played some vital role in the Siege of Boston. Certainly the woman originally bearing it seemed hardly the type to carry old museum tidbits around with her. And I'm sure that Emily Pushing could never be described as an antiquarian, although I believe she fancies herself as rather an expert in the field of milky-white glass—"

"Look, pal," Kilroy interrupted in a patient voice, "you thought out yet how we're going to get at this doctor? We'll be at the Inn in a few minutes—those cops were crazy, you know. There ain't a third the snow over this way we had in Carnavon. Supposing I go in, hey, and ask for the doctor on account of I got this sick uncle of mine out in the car?"

He was so obviously delighted with his suggestion that Leonidas tried to squelch it as gently as he could.

"I'm rather afraid not, Kilroy. You see, in the first place, the doctor's presence is not generally known, and there would be no sound reason for you to ask specifically for him. And in the second place, there is always the very good chance that he may not be a doctor of medicine at all."

"What other kind of doctor could he be, hey?"

"Oh, a corn doctor," Red said, "or an animal doctor, or a dentist."

"Or possibly even a doctor of philosophy." Leonidas ignored Kilroy's start of surprise, and gave him no opportunity to ask if philosophy was sick, hey. "Something about his appearance—principally that brown and white striped suit—makes me very suspicious of assuming that he is a medical doctor. But I suppose you are the one who will have to approach him, Kilroy."

"That's right, pal. This guy might get the wrong angle if Red was to go in and ask for him at this hour of the night!"

"Say, look here!" Red said. "I—"

"Let us," Leonidas went on, "consider the various aspects of the problem. No beguiling notes, definitely. Notes give people too much time in which to think. A telephone message would arouse his suspicions. What I should like would be to get into the Inn and get to him, myself, with Kilroy along to—er—make certain that the doctor gave accurate answers to my questions. But this is hardly fire-escape weather, and I wonder if I—"

"You can't, Mr. Witherall!" Red said flatly. "You can't, and you know it! If they're stopping cars like they stopped us at the Carnavon line, they're hunting for you like crazy! And if this doctor's mixed up in this murder, most likely there'll be a cop or two around. It's too dangerous for you to even get out of the car, let alone to even try sneaking in! And I don't think it's much of a spot to play Army Intelligence, either. What *I* been thinking is, you boys just better sit back and leave this to *me!* I can get him outside and into this car in just about half the time it'd take you to think up some complicated way how to do it!"

While Leonidas knew that what she spoke was the simple truth, he wondered how Kilroy would react to her suggestion.

Before he could frame a tactful question, however, Kilroy began to nod his head slowly.

"She's right, pal. She's the girl can take care of this without no effort or fuss. The desk clerk'll take one gander at her and get the wrong angle, and then call this guy, and *he*'ll get the wrong angle and come down—it's the quickest way. And I'll just hang around to see he don't get too fresh too soon. Say, pal," he added, "what's this guy's name, anyway?"

"Fell," Leonidas told him. "How remiss of me not to have mentioned it before. Doctor B. J. Fell."

"Fell," Kilroy said. "Fell. Doctor Fell. I heard of him somewheres before— I wonder was he in the army, maybe?"

"I think," Leonidas returned, "that you heard the name in an old poem— Red, d'you really feel that you can manage the situation?"

"Listen, Mr. Witherall, don't you worry! I worked a year at the five-and-ten, and a year at the Dalton Tap and Dye, and three joints besides Devlin's Thirty-one Flavors. If I can't handle your corn doctor!"

"She'll be all right, pal," Kilroy assured him calmly. "I taught her jiujitsu before she was fourteen. Now," he pulled the sedan as near to the curb as he could manage, "now, pal, just you sit right here quiet-like and keep that beard of yours out of sight, hey? We'll have your doctor out here for you inside of ten minutes, hey, sugar?"

"Not any longer," Red said confidently. "Gee, I guess you'll have to carry me over to the sidewalk, Kilroy—I can't get over the mounds where they been shovelling. Be careful, Mr. Witherall! Don't talk to any strange cops —or strange girls!"

Leonidas rubbed the steamed window glass with his

forefinger and watched Kilroy deposit Red at the lighted entrance to the Dalton Inn, ahead and to his right.

Then he leaned back against the worn seat cover and tried to relax. He had complete faith in Red's ability to lure Doctor Fell or any other male out into the teeth of an unseasonal November blizzard, and he had complete faith in the phlegmatic Kilroy.

But there was always the octopus of fate!

He told himself sternly to ignore it. Everything was out of his hands. There was nothing he could do. Absolutely nothing!

With his eyes fixed on the Inn's entrance, he forced himself to start reciting "Thanatopsis," as fine a sedative as he knew for the nerves.

Methodically and with infinite accuracy, he recited "Thanatopsis" in its entirety, including the punctuation.

He was grimly starting it all over again when a car swerved diagonally into the curb just ahead of the sedan.

Without muffing a word, Leonidas continued his line. There was nothing in the sight of a convertible beachwagon to make him pause for a moment. Police didn't travel about in heavily chrome-trimmed convertible beachwagons.

But a voice within him screamed out that the girl who brought that bank report, the girl whom Shaver had identified as Fenwick's new secretary, Miss Cowe with an "e," had come to his house in a convertible beachwagon! Mrs. Mullet had said so.

"Comma," Leonidas said. "It would be sheer folly for me to leave this car. 'And sad images of the stern agony comma and shroud comma and pall comma'—oh, it *is* that Cowe girl, she looks exactly like a Powers model, she's blonde, she's beautiful! And—that green tweed outfit from which she's brushing the snow looks as if it might very well match that green pocketbook I found back in Fenwick's library chair!"

To leave this car, the voice within him seemed to be bellowing through a loud-speaker, to leave this car would be the act of an imbecile! Rash, foolhardy, idiotic madness! Incorrigible, irreparable lunacy! No, Mr. Witherall, don't you go tempting the old octopus of fate! Keep right on with "Thanatopsis"!

" 'And breathless darkness comma'! Oh, the chromium buttons on that green topcoat are just exactly like that silly modernistic beetle on that bag's clasp—and I absolutely cannot sit here and prate 'Thanatopsis' to myself! I absolutely must find out what she was doing at Fenwick's, and when she was doing it, and what she knows about—"

Reaching over in the back of the sedan, he grabbed up the green pocketbook and the brown paper package, and thrust open the car door.

Because she was wearing neither overshoes nor rubbers, the girl's progress was slow enough to enable him to catch up with her just as she gingerly stepped up to the revolving door of the Inn.

"I beg your pardon, Miss Cowe!" Leonidas held out the pocketbook. "I believe," he added as she turned around, "that this is yours—"

Uttering a loud, piercing scream, Miss Cowe gave the revolving door a violent shove, and propelled herself into the Inn and out of his sight.

"Say, you, what's the idea?"

Leonidas automatically turned to see who was howling in his ear—and found himself face to face with Sergeant MacCobble.

 ${}^{\text{F}}$OR A STRANGE BEWILDERED MOMENT, the two stood and stared at each other.

"Witherall!" MacCobble said hoarsely. "Witherall!"

As he lunged, Leonidas deftly tripped him, and then he started to run as the sergeant went thudding down in the snow.

Within a scant yard, he abandoned the effort of running in favor of a fast walk.

By the time he managed to reach the corner beyond the Inn, he was happy to stay on his feet at all, and happier to feel that he was making progress in any direction, whether backwards or forwards or sideways.

His moment of happiest triumph, however, arrived when he looked quickly back over his shoulder to discover that Sergeant MacCobble had as yet not been able to effect an upright position.

But his police whistle was shrilling away to the skies.

Leonidas slewed around the corner.

A path had been cleared along the sidewalk of the short side street, but its crusted surface was a treacherous, uneven skating rink over which the snow-crusted soles of Leonidas's leather shoes went sideslipping and skidding.

If he had sensed an aura of "Uncle Tom's Cabin" about his position earlier, when John L. Lewis and the other assorted dogs of Birch Hill Road had been yelping after him, his present plight seemed more of a cross between Eliza crossing the ice floes, and the snowstorm scene of "Way Down East."

"Beset by perilous pitfalls," he muttered to himself as he teetered on one toe in an attempt to regain his faltering balance, "relentlessly driven, the butt of hurtling—ooop!"

He saved himself, and manfully skated on.

If only, he thought, if only he had penned somewhat less ruthless stage directions in those preparatory plans for Haseltine which the fates seemed to have snatched up so gaily and to have followed out so faithfully! He remembered having heard a clock strike eleven just before he began reciting "Thanatopsis" back in Kilroy's car. Actually, therefore, not more than five hours had elapsed since he'd blithely jotted down that clairvoyant data, but he recalled it now as something which he might have written back in the flower of his youth.

He didn't dare risk the chance of falling in order to turn around and see whether or not Sergeant MacCobble was making any headway in his pursuit. But the complete absence of any crunchings and cracklings behind him appeared to indicate that no posse had as yet got organized and under way.

Unless he succumbed to a couple of broken arms or broken ankles—or possibly a broken neck—before he attained the next corner, he was safe. For the next corner lodged the premises of the Dalton Bide-a-Wee Cat and Dog Home, whose front door key, which he had negligently omitted to return when his supervisorship had expired, was even now attached to his key ring. While it was possibly an odd hour of the night for an ex-supervisor to pay a friendly call on his ex-charges, Graves, the caretaker, would doubtless give him shelter. After all, Leonidas thought, it was the usual courtesy which the Home benevolently extended to any passing cat or dog— why not to him?

Then he heard the slap of chains as a car slewed around the corner behind, and he felt his heart sink as the car skidded to a stop just abreast of him.

Of course MacCobble wouldn't have pursued him on foot, Leonidas reflected wearily. MacCobble had his reputation to maintain. MacCobble always arrived first, and by car!

He stopped short.

He had brought all this misfortune on himself when he tempted the old octopus of fate by leaving the sedan to rush in such a foolhardy fashion after the Cowe girl—and one viscous tentacle had promptly smacked him down. There was no earthly sense in his being smacked down a second time and probably crippling himself for life in one final breakneck skate to freedom!

He stood there, waiting for the sergeant to emerge from the coupé.

Then the door swung open.

"Coming, Shakespeare?"

Leonidas felt a sudden upsurge of hope.

"Shaver!" he said. "Shaver!"

He mounted a snowbank, slid down the other side, and tumbled into the coupé.

"Shaver, I thank you!" he said breathlessly as the car started down the street. "Words—words utterly fail me! For the second time, I thank you, Shaver!"

There was an amused chuckle from the coupé's driver

as he swung around the glazed corner by the Bide-a-Wee Home.

"The name is Harriman, Bill Shakespeare. Remember? John, sacked in the Fourth Form, but proud holder of the Founder's Medal for Pleasant Personality and Unremitting Diligence. *That* Harriman."

Leonidas fumbled around in the voluminous folds of Kilroy's polo coat, brought up his pince-nez, and affixed them.

"M'yes, indeed, Harriman!" he said. "Harriman, indeed! Er—for the second time, thank you, Harriman! If I am in any position to have free access to visitors in the next few days, you must remember to drop in and increase my life insurance. I'm not at all sure that I shouldn't also perhaps acquire some sort of new rider on my accident policy, specifically involving mishaps during the pursuit—"

"The pursuit of what?" Harriman inquired as he paused.

"Er—just the pursuit."

"Shakespeare, what the hell is it *this* time? I'd just left a man in the Inn and was starting to go back to the car— I was parked across the street—when all of a sudden I heard a woman screaming and a cop blowing his whistle, and then virtually the entire Dalton police force seemed to be assembling around the Inn entrance, all yelling your name—and I *thought* as I went out that I caught sight of you high-tailing it around the corner. I must admit," he added, "that your high-class surtout threw me for a moment—that polo coat is not, if you don't resent me saying so, the type of garment I personally associate you with. Got your breath? What is it *this* trip?"

"Oh," Leonidas said blandly, "this time the charges are more varied and clear-cut than they were during that earlier, package-snatching episode. I'm wanted for accosting that Cowe girl—"

"*Cow* girl? Comrade, are you quite sober?"

"Cowe with an 'e,' " Leonidas explained. "A girl named Miss Cowe. And then of course they want me for murdering Fenwick Balderston. I dare say by now there must be a host of minor and subsidiary charges, too. Acquiring triplets' cigars under false pretences, impersonating Kilroy's uncle, indecent lurking in Devlin's Thirty-one Flavors, to name a few."

Harriman stopped the car.

"Look," he said anxiously, "they say that Doctor Stinchfield is as good as anyone in Dalton, and he lives just up the street a bit. Now if you have someone you really *prefer* to consult—"

"I've invited one young man to jerk at my beard to prove its authenticity," Leonidas said, "and I might as well invite you to smell my breath to prove my complete sobriety. I have no aches, pains, or funny feelings, of any description, I do not suspect that I am Napoleon, and while I'm reasonably weary from my activities of the evening, I think I may truthfully say that I never thought any more clearly in my life. Er—murdering Fenwick Balderston is, of course, the important charge."

"Murdering Fenwick—Bill Shakespeare, are *you* the one the Frigid News has been blatting about all evening? Are *you* the man with the beard?"

"M'yes—d'you have a radio?" Leonidas inquired. "I'd rather like to hear the latest reports, and—er—shall we perhaps keep moving?"

As he again started up the coupé, Harriman leaned over and punched at buttons on the dashboard.

"There ought to be a Frigid Flash around somewhere," he said. "There practically always is—and it must be around eleven-thirty. Play with it, Shakespeare, and see what you can pick up before I land us in a snowbank."

Leonidas stabbed at the push buttons until he finally located the unctuous voice of Mr. Frigid's announcer.

"Flash! Dalton police have just reported that they now have in their custody Leonidas Witherall, the man with the beard, suspected of murdering Dalton's distinguished citizen, Fenwick Balderston! And now, an extra—a weather flash from Frigid, folks, makers of Frigid's Frozen Foods, the handy, delicious, labor-saving foods that are proving, yes, proving to women all over the country that they, too, can stay young, beautiful, always lovely—when they spare themselves toilsome kitchen drudgery by always using Frigid's Frozen Foods, the deliciously *different* frozen foods! Why spoil lovely hands in preparing carrots, turnips, and other vegetables? Use Frigid's Frozen Foods Delicious Diced Carrots, or Frigid's Frozen Foods Delicious Mashed Turnip, or any of the eighteen other delicious vegetables which make up Frigid—spelled F-r-i-g-i-d—Frigid's Frozen Foods delicious vegetable division! And now for that weather flash! The snow is all over, folks, ha ha ha ha, and from now on, temperatures will moderate rapidly. Slush conditions will, however, generally prevail in most sections. But remember, folks, it's ALWAYS fair weather when you ALWAYS use Frigid's Frozen Foods—and DON'T forget to listen to lovely Bellajeanne Willow, Frigid's Frozen Foods ace food commentator, tomorrow morn—"

Leonidas turned off the radio.

"And," Harriman remarked, "just about high damn time

you did! Some day I must get around to writing my letter to Frigid's God-damned Frozen Foods, assuring them that the avoidance of their product is my life work. Aunt Lil drives miles to get some other brand, she hates that oily announcer so! She—"

"Er—Harriman, are you by some rare chance connected," Leonidas interrupted in the most casual tones, "with the Dalton police?"

"Er—er—er—your*self*, and are you stark raving crazy?" Harriman demanded.

"It's just that I find that I keep asking myself wonderingly," Leonidas said, "what particular Leonidas Witherall the police can have in their custody! Sergeant MacCobble has passed my house roughly twice a day, five days a week, for the last six years. He knows my face and my beard as well as he knows his own father's face—and his beard, if any! I cannot bring myself to believe that the police have some other bearded unfortunate in their clutches, because there is absolutely no possibility of mistaken identity as far as MacCobble is concerned!"

"Oh, probably it was just a premature announcement," Harriman said, "or else that Frigid announcer thought it would be dandy fun to catch you personally before he went off home to bed. Shakespeare, have you any immediate destination?"

"It's imperative that I be in the sedan near the entrance of the Dalton Inn when my good friend Kilroy brings out—"

"Now, now, Bill Shakespeare! None of that Kilroy nonsense!"

"His name is actually not Kilroy," Leonidas said, "he is merely *called* Kil—"

"I know, I know! But on the whole, don't you really think that the whole damn Kilroy business has been pretty well gnawed to the bone?"

"A large youth called Kilroy," Leonidas said with firmness, "and a very lush damsel named Red are both engaged in the chore of securing, for my interrogation, a person I rather suspect of being an important factor in the murder of Fenwick Balderston."

"Oh? Is it," Harriman inquired drily, "anyone we know?"

"A Doctor Fell."

"Doctor Fell, Doctor Fell—you know, Bill, I seem to have heard that name before!"

"M'yes, of course you have. 'I do not love thee, Doctor Fell,'" he quoted, "And so on. Everyone including the excellent Kilroy has heard that name before!"

"You think this Fell fellow—and I'm not trying to pun! —killed Balderston? Say, Bill, what *happened* after I left you there at Ironmongery Manor, anyway? How in hell did you come to get mixed up with all this?"

"When I went in, I found Fenwick dead on the library floor," Leonidas said, "and someone had thoughtlessly utilized a former gift paperweight of mine as a murder weapon. At that time, my serious involvement in the affair seemed a foregone conclusion, although I have lived to learn that there are numerous other complicating factors —including, as I said, this Doctor Fell."

Harriman drove along silently for several moments.

"Look," he said at last, "this is none of my damn business, and I probably shouldn't attempt to offer any constructive thoughts to my elders and betters, but—*why* in hell do you go tearing around one half a jump ahead of the cops? You never killed this Balderston character, and you know it! Why don't you just go tell the cops all, and wash it all up? Of course," a note of irony crept into his voice, "I wasn't at Meredith's *too* long, but I *seem* to remember some tidbit carved over the front door—something to do with the truth, as I recall—now just *how* did it go? Tell the truth, and you'd never, never have to cheese it from the cops, or *some*thing like that?"

"*Touché*," Leonidas said. "*Touché!* M'yes. If the old octopus of fate had not chosen to—er—enmesh me in a rather weird sequence of events, if I had not fecklessly run when I should valiantly have stood, if I had not tripped Sergeant MacCobble just now, if, indeed, I had only myself to consider, I might very possibly have flung myself on the tender mercies of the police. I could, of course, even now do so. But there is a project involving Meredith's which is very dear to my heart, and this paralyzing bolt of adverse publicity will ruin it forever if I do not counteract it by achieving something spectacular in the line of amateur detective work. In a nutshell, it is my very firm intention to unearth Fenwick Balderston's murderer by myself. At that point, I shall willingly and happily—er—tell the cops all."

The coupé, which had been making only moderate progress according to the standards of Kilroy, perceptibly slowed its speed.

"No! Oh, no, Bill Shakespeare!"

"M'yes," Leonidas said evenly. "Er—quite definitely yes. I have been successful several times before in this sort of thing, you know."

Harriman chuckled, and the car picked up speed again.

"Well," he said, "I suppose you know your own

strength, but you won't mind my saying that to me it seems like rather a lost cause, will you? And now—of course you *can't* return to the Dalton Inn to meet this Kilroy character! Not unless you cut off your beard and go in blackface! Look here, Bill Shakespeare, exactly what *are* you going to do? Exactly where *would* it be safe for you to go?"

"Where," Leonidas returned, "would it be quite convenient for you to leave me? After all, my dear fellow, I hardly expect you to ferry me about indefinitely in the pursuit of my lost cause, and—"

"Listen!" Harriman interrupted hotly, "I didn't mean that I thought you *could*n't solve this thing, I only meant—"

"That you didn't think that I *could*. M'yes," Leonidas said with a smile. "I quite understand. Japing aside, however, I'm not unaware of the dangers you run in transporting me, and it is not my desire to involve you in this imbroglio in any way. Suppose that you drop me off on the next corner, by the bus stop, where—"

"*Never!*" Harriman interrupted again. "I will *not!* Why, Bill, I never in my life heard such childish, idiotic prattle! Do I gather that you're nursing some mad notion of taking a *bus* back downtown, back to the Dalton Inn to meet your Kilroy friend? Why, you—you—look, even if the busses were running, you couldn't go back! You can't!"

"The snow has stopped as Mr. Frigid predicted," Leonidas said calmly, "the busses will soon be running again, and actually, I intend to go to the Bide-a-Wee Home and—"

"And play with the dear little stray kitties, I suppose?" Harriman reached heights of irony.

"And wait there," Leonidas continued imperturbably, "until the Dalton police grow weary—as they ultimately will—of the Dalton Inn and its vicinity, and go elsewhere. I wish," he added, "I *do* wish that I could think what Red and Kilroy will do when they discover that I have vanished! But Red is an ingenious child, and I suspect that somehow we will achieve some liaison, somehow! If they find it unwise or imprudent to remain near the Inn, Red will doubtless figure out some way in which to leave a message for me—"

" 'Kilroy was here!' " Harriman broke in. "Of course! It's a natural!"

"It is indeed! M'yes, I think you'd best drop me off, Harriman. I'll make out."

"You seem," Harriman said, "so damn sure!"

"Whereas I have not precisely told the truth," Leonidas said lightly, "I fear no man."

"But my God, Shakespeare, suppose that you *should* stumble onto something hot? What then, my fine Bard of Avon? You're not going to be playing marbles for fun, you know! You'll be playing for keeps—and with a murderer! And if he can do it once, he can do it again!"

"M'yes, he *can* do it again," Leonidas returned, "but this man is far too intelligent, I suspect, to take any such completely fatal step."

"Oh? And how do you figure that out?"

"One murder," Leonidas said, "is a single pencil dot on a large sheet of white paper. You and I can draw random lines from any direction to that little dot, but we'll never *know* if our points of departure are within a million miles of the truth. We're merely punching our fists into ice cream, we're grappling with handfuls of mist. But another murder—ah, another murder is another pencil point, and any small and not very bright child can with ease draw a line between two dots!"

That was the airy sort of commentary, Leonidas thought with a slight start of shame, which Haseltine characters with intellectual pretensions were always bringing forth. He was, in fact, almost quoting verbatim from some old book whose plot and title alike had long since evaporated from his memory.

To turn and find Harriman nodding serious agreement to his words, which he himself considered both a little fatuous and not particularly rational, came as somewhat of a shock.

"But," he went on quickly, to cover his surprise, "but I digress. Er—I note that we're getting farther and farther from the center of the town. May I ask where you are headed?"

"I'm going to the Country Club," Harriman said, "and unless you kick and scream too violently, I think you'd better come along with me—no, wait, and let me explain. After I left you at Ironclad Castle, I had some assorted chores to do for Aunt Lil—that's my aunt, Mrs. Rumford, you know, the one I live with. I was setting out to do them, as a matter of fact, when you barged into the driveway way back there when. She's the head of some doings or other they're having at the club, and of course after I did her little errands—collecting extra card tables and bridge lamps, and all such—I got roped in to take care of all the other odds and ends that'd gone wrong. You know—"

"M'yes, I do. The ice cream, of course, failed to arrive," Leonidas said, "and the man with the gilt chairs didn't come."

"Shakespeare, you're psychic! I located the ice cream— the boy driving the truck had just stopped off to help his girl with her algebra, a mere detour of eleven miles—and I got the gilt chairs. Then I found Blinko, no mean achievement!"

"Blinko," Leonidas said interestedly, "is an absolutely new character to me. Is he a floor-waxer or a piano player?"

"He's a magician. 'Refined gatherings a specialty,' his card says. Blinko went on to Daltonville instead of getting off his train at Dalton Hills—a little phonetic problem," Harriman said, "arising from Aunt Lil's never talking directly into a telephone receiver. She's always too busy with other things that catch her attention just as someone answers. Then I found the piano player, and replaced a few fuses—"

"M'yes, indeed! The east wing invariably blows."

"Shakespeare, is it second sight?"

"Er—no. I was Chairman of the House Committee during the war, when all the rest of Dalton's available manpower either was in the service or in Washington. I know," Leonidas said with pride, "exactly what to do when the kitchen drain stops up, and I am magnificent on the west wing's plumbing. Mr. Bagliotti, the roofer, offered me a job after my masterly diagnosis of the source of the dining room ceiling leak!"

"Next time Aunt Lil runs one of these barbecues with imported talent and spun sugar," Harriman said, "you are my boy! Well, it began snowing before I finished with the fuses, and then all of a sudden the first batch of people were starting to leave—and of course their cars were either snowed in, or frozen up, or slightly glacéed. And of course it hadn't occurred to anyone to provide themselves with rubber boots or overshoes, or mittens, or earlaps, or heavy coats—oh, Shakespeare," he began to laugh, "you never saw a lovelier sight!"

His laughter was so infectious that Leonidas found himself chuckling.

"Those women!" Harriman went on. "Hopping like fat sparrows through the snow! Squealing about their ruined slippers, and keening about their ruined dresses—a lot of 'em were pretty elegant and bouffante, if that's the proper word! And all those old boys in boiled shirts getting all soppy and red-faced! And their studs popping! And if anyone did manage to break a car loose, they just went piling up on that grade leading out of the parking space driveway!"

"And no one thought of the skis and the snowshoes and all the winter sports equipment—including clothes and boots—packed away in the south shed?" Leonidas inquired. "Or remembered the sleighs down in the old barn? Or considered the possibility of hitching them up to Molly and Myrna, the horses who served us so faithfully during the non-mechanized war years?"

"No one remembered anything, or thought of anything —or *had* anything! You'd think a brisk touch of winter was some strange new phenomenon in New England, the way they all went carrying on! No one had chains stowed away in their cars—except me!—and few had anti-freeze, even," Harriman said, "no one had a towrope, no one knew where there might be snow shovels stored away—"

"D'you mean," Leonidas interrupted, "that after all the furious fanfare attending our purchase of a brand-new little tractor plough, no one had sense enough to utilize it? I am intensely depressed, Harriman, intensely depressed!"

Harriman snorted.

"And how do you think *I* feel, to learn all these things *now?* Because, having chains, *I* was the lad, Shakespeare, who drove to town and bought up all available supplies, and brought them back with two garage men I lured with promises of vast rewards. Then I started ferrying the more timorous spirits home—I never suspected Aunt Lil had so many female friends who were spinsters, or widows, or just unattached, and afraid of the dark if it contained a few snowflakes. So I—what are you roaring your head off about, anyway?"

"I'm thinking," Leonidas said, "of the Club's Motor Corps and Mobile Canteen, run and managed during the war by those same unattached females, and how neither rain nor hail nor gloom of night kept them from the swift completion of their appointed rounds, hurtling coffee and doughnuts and goodies the length and breadth of the state, usually in weather which would have caused the average sensible polar bear to shiver in fright. Ah, the toys of peace!"

"If I thought for one moment," Harriman retorted, "that you were telling the truth about those gals, and not just trying to goad me, I'd be very sorely tempted to collect them and take them all right *back* to the club! Well, anyway, I'd just finished dumping a little load of 'em in the Centre, and leaving poor stranded Blinko at the Inn, when bang! I connected with you again. I've got another group waiting—Shakespeare, I can't get the notion out of my head that you shouldn't tackle this Balderston business! At least, you shouldn't try to tackle it all by your little lonesome self!"

"When any individual becomes as violently enmeshed with the old octopus of fate as I currently am," Leonidas said, "it would be sheer, utter folly to attempt a withdrawal. It simply is not possible. While I greatly appreciate your solicitude for my welfare, I have no other course."

"You make it all seem," Harriman remarked, "like that group of statuary—you know, those three gigantic men all wrapped up in snakes, writhing in horrible agony. What's the name of the thing?"

"Er—Laocoön," Leonidas told him. "M'yes. Merely substitute the viscous tentacles of a fateful octopus, and you have an approximation of my general appearance and position at this moment. Now, Harriman, if you have still more stranded females to ferry home, perhaps you'd best just leave me at the end of the bus line, don't you think? I really *must* get—"

"Wait, Shakespeare, I'm only finally arriving at the point I set out to make when I started telling about my gay night life at the swank Dalton Country Club, as the *Chronicle* loves to call it. I've only three more women to ferry—all dear pals of Aunt Lil's—and Lil herself. I can make one trip of it, with a little judicious sardining. Now here's my bright thought—while I cope with them, *you* stay at the club—"

"Er no, Harriman!" Leonidas interrupted with some firmness. "No, really, I fear I cannot—"

"Oh, I don't mean stay, as sit down and make yourself at home in the billiard room! I mean, suppose you hole up in some obscure corner of the joint, which you seem to know like the palm of your hand, while I get those gals out of the way. Then, see, I'll come back and pick you up, and we can sally forth, and try to make connections with your friends at the Inn, or whatever you want to do. What's the name of that Haseltine-to-the-Rescue fellow's devoted slave? Oh, *you* wouldn't know, of course, but it's Faithful Someone—Faithful Freddie, Faithful Ferdy—"

"Faithful Frank, I believe," Leonidas said.

"That's it! Well, if you must play Haseltine, you'd better let me play Frank. I don't think it's safe for you to go ripping around by yourself! How about it, Shakespeare? You might just as well park at the club as with the Bide-a-Wee's stray pups!"

"I suppose," Leonidas said reflectively, "I suppose—m'yes, perhaps the club *is* as satisfactory a place as any!"

"At least there's no chance of your picking up distemper," Harriman said as he started the car up the hill toward the club, "or fleas. I won't be very long. You can spend the interval usefully brooding—you know, like a detective in a book."

"M'yes, quite."

"Apply the mind," Harriman went on, "in the old Meredith manner. 'Steady, stubborn application to the problem in hand is the basic root of true success in life.' I once wrote that, or something very like it, two hundred times on the blackboard of the Lower School study."

"I wish," Leonidas seemed almost to be speaking to himself, "I wish I could figure out how to locate Kilroy and Red, and discover—"

"Every time you bring up that name Kilroy, this whole

business suddenly seems unreal!" Harriman waited for a departing car to inch its way past them on the curve outside the club's front gates. "*Kil*roy, yet!"

"I must discover what they did with Fell, after they—m'yes, perhaps it will be an excellent idea for me to sit down and engage in some useful brooding! I'm going to slip over to the caddy house, Harriman, and brood there with great vigor until you return for me."

"But it'll be locked—how can you get in? Or do you always carry a jimmy as standard equipment?"

"I have a master key," Leonidas told him with a smile. "Gold-plated, and tastefully engraved with a touching tribute to my four years in the House Committee trenches. Now that I think of it, they told me at the presentation that I could go anywhere at all in the club at any time the spirit moved me!"

"Shakespeare," Harriman said tentatively as he swung into the parking space, "Shakespeare—"

"Er—yes?—merciful heavens!" Leonidas surveyed the networks of jagged ruts and the piles of snow. "What chaotic turmoil there must have been here! Something of an Iwo Jima at the South Pole!"

"One of Aunt Lil's friends said it looked as if a giant had chewed up mouthfuls of snow and then spat them back again—but the place is practically cleaned out, now! You should have seen it when!"

"Have people simply gone away and abandoned all these remaining cars?" Leonidas asked curiously.

"Some were waiting for the snow to stop, some are waiting for chains or chauffeurs or general reinforcements, and some said they'd pick 'em up in the first thaw." Harriman laughed. "I even heard one old boy announce that his damn car could damn well stay there till he damn well came back from Florida in May—Shakespeare, will you tell me something I've been dying to know? *Why* in hell are you still carrying that silly little brown paper package with you? *And* the lady's pocketbook?"

"At this point," Leonidas said, "largely from sheer force of habit. Ah, I see that there's a path beaten out to the east porch, and it's only a step from there to the caddy house—"

"Don't you think," Harriman started to get out, "that Faithful Frank should perhaps reconnoiter?"

"I hardly think," Leonidas said, "that any patrol project will be necessary!"

"I don't see anyone, either—and say, how's for my extra pair of overshoes? They're not really mine, they were given me for somebody's husband, but I lost track of who."

"Whom," Leonidas corrected him automatically. "Thank you, I'd be most grateful for them."

When he stepped out of the coupé a few minutes later, wearing the overshoes which were a full size too large, he overheard Harriman's subdued chuckle.

"I can't help it, Shakespeare! If you were only standing where I am, you'd howl, too! You couldn't help—oops, watch those coat skirts! If you could only see yourself, with that—that—oh, *will* you tell me where you picked up that super-duper bathrobe of a coat?"

"It's Kilroy's." Leonidas reached in the car and took out his package and the pocketbook.

"*That* I can believe! If ever a garment was built for Kilroy, that coat was! Say, Shakespeare! *Shake*speare!"

"Please!" Leonidas said gently. "If you wouldn't yell

out what amounts to my nickname in *quite* such a vociferous fashion!"

"But look—I just thought! Blinko! *That's* the answer, Blinko! Don't you see?"

"Er—no, Harriman, frankly, I'm afraid that I don't."

"Blinko was stranded here by the storm—no one could guess when or if trains or busses would be running into Boston, so I took him to the Dalton Inn—don't you get it?" Harriman demanded excitedly. "He has a beard, and he was wearing a polo coat! *He's* the one who the cops got!"

"Whom, Harriman. *Whom!*"

"Who, whom, what does it matter which? The point is, the cops must have grabbed him in the lobby of the Dalton Inn—and *that's* why they reported having you in custody! And now, for God's sakes, be *careful*, Bill Shakespeare! Stay there quietly in the caddy house until Faithful Frank comes—just don't let yourself get into any more crazy trouble, will you?"

"I promise," Leonidas said, "to be a very good boy!"

The Blinko theory, he thought as he walked rapidly past the east porch and around the corner to the caddy house, was an excellent theory.

Except that he knew perfectly well that Sergeant Mac-Cobble would never be fooled for ten seconds by Blinko, or by any other reasonable facsimile of himself.

Could someone on the Dalton force have been inspired to give out a false report of his arrest in order to lure him out into the open?

Leonidas shook his head as he fumbled for his key ring.

"Could MacCobble—" he murmured.

No, MacCobble could not! MacCobble admittedly had

occasional flights of fancy, but he couldn't possibly have been inspired to that desirable extent!

The moon was beginning to shine again now in the cleared sky, and by its wan light he finally located the gold-plated master key. Then, after scuffling the snow on the threshold aside with his borrowed boots, he opened the caddy house door.

The golf professional or one of his assistants must have been working out in the rear shop sometime during the afternoon, he decided, for the main room was warm, as if the heat had been on.

Leonidas loosened Kilroy's coat, put his package and the pocketbook down on one of the wooden benches, and sat down on another. He wouldn't of course dare to put on a light, but he really didn't require one. A little of the moonlight filtered in, and the far windows picked up some of the glow from the east porch lights.

He really needed this period of quiet meditation. He needed to sort out some of the miscellaneous details that had cropped up by the wayside.

But first of all, he needed to think out the problem of Doctor Fell.

What *would* have happened when Kilroy and Red brought the man out and found the sedan empty?

"Devoutly and from the bottom of my heart, I wish I could guess!" he said aloud. "And I wish I could guess where they are now!"

And he wished that he knew what had become of Shaver.

And always in the background fringes of his mind lurked those idiot details of the monkey eating the Delicious apple, and the quart of ice cream, and the mink coat that had all vanished into the blue.

And *was* there a little milliner in Fenwick's apparently impeccable life?

Or two little milliners?

Or three?

Leonidas devoted a cheerful moment to the consideration of a long, long line of little milliners, alternately blonde and brunette, each carrying a hatbox in either hand, and wearing a mink coat on the shoulder of which a monkey perched, madly chewing at a bright red apple.

And that Miss Cowe—why had she uttered that unearthly scream at his appearance? While he judged from Harriman's taunts that he was no Cornel Wilde, neither was he any Boris Karloff!

But the Fell problem came first.

He remembered suddenly that there was a telephone back in the professional's workshop, and he wondered if it were still an extension from the club's main line, as it had been during the war, or if it had been changed back to a regular, direct, outgoing wire.

If he could only call up the Dalton Inn and ask for Doctor Fell, Leonidas thought, he might at least learn whether the man was out—and presumably still in the clutches of Kilroy and Red—or in—in which event he could fabricate a Doctor Bell or Pell with whom the desk clerk should have connected him, and hang up.

He got up and made his way through the caddy room into the workshop, congratulating himself the while on his masterly progress in the dimness.

Then he stumbled against a bag of golf clubs which

145

fell to the floor with a bang and a clatter, and in drawing back from them, he bumped his elbow against a table.

At once, apparently with the cooperation of the octopus of fate, dozens of golf balls started to fall on the floor in the corner.

While they thudded and clicked and plopped and bounced and rolled, Leonidas stood there helplessly, half-expecting that at any instant crowds would come rushing down from the club to investigate the noise.

Then he told himself firmly that no one could possibly have heard a thing from that distance, and continued on to the phone only to find the line as dead as a doornail.

Probably the fault of the storm, he decided with regret.

He picked his way with care as he went back through the workshop. While his eyes were now thoroughly accustomed to the light—or rather to the lack of it—he mistrusted what his elbows and the skirts of Kilroy's coat might do to a lathe or to one of the electric motors.

In the doorway to the caddy room, he stopped short.

Someone was sitting on the bench which he had just left.

A WOMAN.

A hatless woman, in a fur coat and an evening dress that swirled in billowing folds onto the caddy room floor.

"Er—good evening," Leonidas said courteously. "Are you looking for the professional, or—er—do you wish a caddy, perhaps?"

"I wish," the woman had a pleasant, low voice, "my dinosaur's footprint."

"Doubtless it is the acoustics," Leonidas said, "but it rather sounded as if you wished—er—a dinosaur's footprint."

"Exactly."

"A dinosaur's *foot*print?"

"Not 'a.' 'My.' "

"M'yes," Leonidas said blandly. "Of course! Not *a* dinosaur's footprint. *My* dinosaur's footprint. M'yes, indeed! Permit me to say, madam, that nothing would enchant me more than to provide you with your dinosaur's footprint—if you will only be good enough to provide me with the dinosaur!"

"You had it," the woman said simply. "Where is it?"

"It was my feeble impression," Leonidas stepped from the doorway and sat down on a bench opposite her, "that I knew all the games which the members of this club, sober or otherwise, could concoct. This dinosaur's footprint game, however, is obviously something quite new, and possibly a very logical outgrowth of the events of the evening. Do I guess something, or finish a last line? 'I wish my dinosaur's footprint'—"

"And I do, too!"

"Really," Leonidas peered vainly at the woman's face in an effort to recognize her, "really, nothing *rhymes* with it, you know, and I speak as one who's rather good at that sort of thing. 'I wish my dinosaur's footprint.' You'd have to finish out the line, obviously. 'I wish'—I offer this merely as an extemporaneous example, of course—'I wish my dinosaur's footprint were *here*'—hm. Here. Near. Ah, yes. 'I wish my dinosaur's footprint were *near*.' Now I have it! 'I wish it would *stay*, Not go wandering *away*, I wish my dinosaur's print would ap*pear!*' "

"If it isn't here and near," the woman said, "and if you can't make it appear, I *do* wish you'd tell me what you did with it! Because it simply *has* to be in the air express tonight—oh. D'you suppose there'll *be* air express with the storm?"

"While I am no meteorologist," Leonidas leaned back, convinced that he had never seen this woman before in his life, "Mr. Frigid announced some half hour ago that the storm was all over, and that clearing and slush would promptly take place. Not as concisely as that, of course, the information was sandwiched in between many delicious carrots and lovely, lovely hands—er—do you invariably air express all your dinosaur's footprints?"

"When I have them to express! Really, where *is* it?"

"Dear lady, I wish I knew! But I assure you that the location of your dinosaur or his footprint is a matter concerning which I am in complete if regretful ignorance.

And I might add in passing that traces of an extinct gigantic reptile are virtually all that I *have* missed, to-night!"

"But you took it!"

"*I* took it?"

"You certainly did! You—"

"Truly," Leonidas said gently, "truly, I fear that you are harboring the erroneous illusion that I am Blinko, the conjurer, the prestidigitator, the master of legerdemain. Er—'Refined gatherings a specialty.' If Blinko pilfered your dinosaur's footprint in some moment of magical abandon, he doubtless has it with him at the Dalton Inn, where he is spending the ni—"

"You took it! You *snatched* it from me—"

"Oh!" Leonidas whipped on his pince-nez. "*Oh!*"

"And ran like a madman—"

"Oh! M'yes, indeed! *That* dinosaur's footprint!" Leonidas made a rapid recovery. "The dinosaur's footprint in the little brown paper package addressed to Emily Pushing! But of course, of course! So it *did* pertain more nearly to Cro-Magnon man than to the Siege of Boston, or a flower pot, or rubble! To be sure, to be sure! Why didn't you say so at *once?* I didn't understand that you were referring to *that* dinosaur's footprint!"

"It seems to me," the woman returned, "that I worked my little fingers to the bone trying to get the idea across to you! Where is it now?"

Leonidas arose.

"By the merest happy chance," he said, "you are now practically sitting on it. It's right here on the end of the bench, beside that pocketbook. Permit me to return it to you—and I can't begin to tell you how very happy and delighted I am to see that dinosaur's footprint restored to its rightful owner. Er—you *are* its rightful owner, I trust?"

"I have a bill of sale at home, but if you doubt me, you can always wade up to the club house and ask Emily Pushing for details. She's spent the better part of the night telling everyone about my purchase, and I'm sure she'd simply adore telling *you!*"

"Oh, I'm sure she would!" Leonidas said heartily. "There's nothing Emily adores more than telling—it's unquestionably the supreme goal of her life, with seeing people running a very close second. Only—"

"Only what?" she asked as he paused.

"Only it's one of my supreme goals," he went on, "never to permit Emily Pushing—or anyone resembling her— even the slightest opportunity to tell me anything. Perhaps, therefore, under the circumstances, you would consent to—er—clarify the situation yourself?"

The woman laughed delightedly.

"Oh, Bill!" she said. "You simply haven't changed a single bit!"

"Indeed?" Leonidas found himself suddenly yearning to turn on the light and take a good look at this woman who seemed to know him so well—well enough, at least, to know that he looked like Shakespeare, and to call him Bill without any of the usual, forcedly humorous preambles. "Er—really?"

"And I was *so* afraid you would be different!" she said. "That's why I went peering in your windows back on Birch Hill Road, you know, and getting stuck in your evergreens, and losing my pump, and all!"

"Really!" Leonidas wondered how Kilroy would handle this occasion of some unremembered female re-entering his life. But a chipper "Say, pal, who in hell are you?" seemed hardly the tactful solution.

"I'd been at Emily's—how *do* you describe that stucco edifice of theirs, Bill?"

"In my mind," Leonidas almost felt relieved to meet her on the neutral ground of architecture, "I have always thought of it as Early Roosevelt By-Pass French-Pseudish. I dare say that some archeologist of the future will footnote it even more specifically, as 'The Green Glasswalled Bathroom Era,' or 'First Phase W.P.A.—Create Work at Any Price.'"

She nodded. "That's good. Bastard French Variegated was as far as I could get. Well, I'd been at Emily's buying that fool footprint—I'd *just* missed it at that auction at Pomfret this afternoon, you see," she explained. "By ten minutes. We took a wrong turn, and when we finally got to the sale, the footprint had already been sold. And what an utterly hellish time I had tracking down who'd bought it! 'Mrs. Pushing' conveyed absolutely nothing to me! I never had any idea she'd turn out to be Emily Smellie, of all people!"

"Er—Emily *Who?*"

"She *was* Emily Smellie, you see, when she and I were at boarding school together. At Miss Clinch's."

"And to think," Leonidas began a methodical mental survey of every woman he had ever known who had attended Miss Clinch's, "to think I've always been convinced that Emily Pushing could not possibly be improved upon as a definitive name! But—er—don't you find Pushing singularly appropriate, too?"

151

"It's so utterly wonderful that if she had any sense of humor at all, I'd suspect her of marrying Yeoville solely for his name!" she giggled. "And she believes so intensely in Dalton, The Garden City, and Birch Hill Road, A Lovely Neighborhood, and in her Pseudish house, and in Yeoville—isn't Yeoville *awful?*"

"He has better teeth."

"*Better*, d'you think," she said critically, "or just *fewer?* Well, anyway, amid much gay reunioning on her part, I bought the dinosaur's footprint from her. She really didn't want to part with it one bit, you know, I only broke her down by sheer force of personality—and the incidental offer of a huge profit. And she ran on about her Nice Neighbors, in capitals, and named and placed them one by one. I was simply pining to know if Leonidas Witherall was actually you, so on the way back past your house, I went and peeked in. And lost my pump in your evergreens, and then that girl came *flying* out—"

"Er—*girl?*" Leonidas interrupted blankly.

"Yes. I thought it rather odd."

"I think it rather odd, too," Leonidas said. "Could you, d'you suppose, give me a thumbnail description of her? Say a few hundred concise words?"

"She simply *flew* out, and I was busy trying to locate my pump—don't worry, Bill, I'm sure I'll never recognize her again!"

"It is not my desire to cover up this visitor of mine," Leonidas said, "but to bring her to light. She was a burglar, you know."

"Oh?"

"M'yes. She'd stolen from my house a brown paper-wrapped package which contained a bank report and which was an exact duplicate of your dinosaur's foot-print package in size, shape and thickness. It even bore a similar label from the Dalton Safe Deposit and Trust. Er —did Emily wrap up the footprint for you?"

"Oh, my, yes! After much excited hooting around in closets by Yeoville, and much dragging out of lower desk drawers for a bit of suitable wrapping, Emily finally contributed the brown paper that her brand-new check-book was done up in. Yeoville said it was pretty smart of her, what?" With a trick of intonation, she deftly paro-died Yeoville's hearty, booming voice. "He said they really ought to keep a special stock of paper on hand just for emergencies, like doing up dinosaur's footprints, ha ha ha!"

"I see!" Leonidas said. "And now perhaps you under-stand why, when I saw you later, I snatched your package from you. Of course I thought that it was *my* package, and that *you* were responsible for its theft. Did you—er —see me come out of my house shortly after this flying girl departed?"

She hesitated.

"Yes," she said at last. "Yes. I saw you. But I—well, I was in such a damned silly position, Bill, wedged in among your evergreens with one pump off and one pump on! Very, very definitely not at my best! I really couldn't bring myself to come hobbling out with a merry expla-nation about how I just happened to be peeking in at you in a wave of nostalgia—*not* with one pump off! And besides, if young girls found it necessary to *flee* from you—"

She left the rest of the sentence poised insinuatingly in mid-air.

"I resent that!" Leonidas said promptly. "It's a thoroughly unwarranted, unjustified, unmerited and undeserved assumption. *Why?*"

"Why should I have assumed it? Why *not?*" she retorted. "Emily had just told me you were terribly intellectual but terribly, terribly eccentric—and then ten minutes later, I see young girls rushing from your house in headlong flight! And—"

"A girl," Leonidas interrupted. "Not *girls!*"

"And then you went marching away, apparently after your girl, and I unearthed my pump, and left—and the next thing *I* knew, you'd sneaked up on me like a—a common footpad, and snatched my package! And at that point, I blew my whistle for the boys!" she concluded. "I decided you were just a wee bit too eccentric for me to cope with by myself!"

Leonidas thoughtfully twirled his pince-nez on their broad black ribbon.

"M'yes," he said, "I think that I can perhaps concede your—er—points. Of course it's admittedly none of my business, but tell me—*why* was your car parked around the corner at such a great distance from your destination? And—"

Before he could add a tentative, tactful inquiry about those two uniformed giants whom she had so lightly referred to as the boys, she began to laugh.

"Oh, that *car!* I always leave it well out of sight whenever I plan to buy anything," she said. "Always. Just a glimpse of it brings out the worst of everyone's inflationary tendencies—why, *think* how Emily Pushing would have soaked me for the dinosaur's footprint if she'd had a look at that car first! I loathe the thing, but there's not

154

much I can do about it. Now you tell *me*," she went on rather hurriedly, "how did you get away from the boys, and the dogs, and the assorted neighbors, back there on Birch Hill Road? In that coupé that pulled out of a driveway, as I suspected?"

"M'yes. I'm ashamed to say—er—really, my face burns, but—er—"

It had been his intention to tell her about his ignominious retreat from the vicinity of Birch Hill Road on the floor of Harriman's car, but she chose to put a different interpretation on his hesitancy.

"D'you mean to say that at long last you're going to break down and put an end to this refined skirmishing, and actually confess that you haven't the remotest idea who I am?" she demanded.

"Certainly not!" Leonidas lied stoutly. "Your name is on the tip of my tongue! I merely felt that since you had originated this—er—this masquerade in the first place," he was fighting for time, but he had a hopeless feeling that if she hadn't dropped any clews by now, she probably never would, "you naturally wished me to keep it up to the bitter end. Therefore—"

"Stop stalling, Bill! You don't know me! And after all the clews I've thrown at you!"

She was a contemporary of Emily Pushing's, she had attended Miss Clinch's School, she was obviously younger than himself. Clews. Clews? *Clews?* Leonidas thought desperately. She bought a secondhand dinosaur's footprint from Emily, she lost a pump in his evergreens— had he ever known any woman anywhere who went around buying dinosaur's footprints? Never! Any woman who went around losing pumps? Losing pumps! Now who was it who always lost a pump at some critical moment?

Eureka!

"My dear Liz Copley," he said blandly, "you had no need to throw clews at me! I'm only trying to tell you how ashamed I am not to be able to remember your husband's name!"

"I'm not at all certain that it wasn't some sudden inspiration," she returned with more than a touch of intuition. "But you're luckier than you might guess, Bill! In case no one ever bothered telling you, the one sure way to earn a woman's undying fury is to forget her name after asking her to marry you!"

"I was plagued," Leonidas felt as though a balky parachute had opened at the last moment and deposited him on a feather bed, "by the etiquette of the situation, Liz. Er—should one remember a girl one asked to marry one who almost the next moment eloped with—oh, dear, he wore glasses and was known as a hustler, and his name was Joe!"

"George!"

"His name," Leonidas said, "is of far less importance than the fact that I was, of course, prostrated by the whole heart-rending business. For many, many weeks, I was shattered. A broken thing."

"My mother," Liz said skeptically, "wrote me that you congratulated her warmly on her new son-in-law, and she claimed to have detected a strong undercurrent of relief in your voice. I don't re*call* her mentioning that you took to your bed with grief, or went into any wasting declines!"

"Liz," Leonidas felt that it was time to change the subject, "how in the world did you manage to track me and the dinosaur's footprint to this place? Tracking down Emily Pushing from a Pomfret auction is one thing, but finding me here is utterly beyond my comprehension!"

She laughed, and lighted a cigarette she took out of a small handbag.

"Actually, Bill, I'd given you up—except for composing in my mind a little gem of a letter demanding the instant return of the dinosaur's footprint, or else! In fact, I was even dallying with the nasty thought of sending my attorney to call on you in person. Finding you here was sheer luck."

"Oh?" Leonidas said. "You mean that you often drop into caddy houses at midnight after blizzards, just on the off chance of running into someone who's stolen your dinosaur's footprint?"

"Don't be idiotic! I mean that I'm waiting here for my niece to pick me up," Liz said, "and that I've *been* waiting for years and years—I suppose the child's probably stuck in a drift somewhere. Anyway, I got so bored with Emily and Yeoville and their jolly friends—"

"Exactly what *was* going on here tonight?" Leonidas interrupted.

"It was a 'Do-What-You-Want' evening. A sort of combination three-ring circus and musicale and bridge, with dancing, and in theory you picked what you wished to do. There was Blinko, in installments, and sandwiched in between his acts was a group who sang songs in hoopskirts, and then in wimples, and then in bathing suits—*you* know. And a woman with a harp, and a soprano—"

"Did she pin ap-pils to a li-lock tree?" Leonidas inquired. "Or was she the blonde one who renders gems from the works of Nole Card?"

"From—? Oh. Yes, she rent Nole limb from limb! Blinko was perfectly lovely," Liz said, "but I found the rest a little fatiguing. And I got stuck with Emily and Yeoville, who hardly let me out of their clutches all night. But I finally broke away from them and trudged down to the parking space to see if there was anyone who could give me a lift, or if I could grab the next taxi—and I was frozen to the bone, so I hopped into a car. It just happened to be the sedan parked next to that coupé you came in."

"Oh."

"And following you *here* was simple enough," Liz went on, "and you very conveniently covered my entrance with a lot of noise." She dropped her cigarette on the floor and carefully stepped on it. "And that is how Granny once again found her dinosaur's footprint!"

"And you—er—heard our conversation out by the car, I presume?"

"Most of it."

Leonidas thought he began to understand why she had not at once demanded, or put on, a light.

"And you are—er—aware that I find myself in a slight predicament?"

"No. What I gathered," Liz said, "was that you were in the hell of a mess."

"Perhaps," Leonidas said, "that *is* a more accurate appraisal. M'yes."

"*I* think so. And," Liz said, "somehow you didn't sound to me out there like someone girls flee from, or like a man who goes around making a habit of snatching dinosaur's footprints from defenseless women—I might add, Bill, that while I knew perfectly well who you were, back there on Birch Hill Road, I didn't tell either your neighbors or that lovely fat policeman who wanted your description. The boys and I said you were a tall dark man, and never mentioned your beard. So no one knows. Now —what *is* this mess? What's happened, and *why* are you hiding in this dreary place?"

"I'm killing time until Harriman—that young fellow who brought me in the coupé—returns," Leonidas said. "And I can't imagine what's keeping him, unless he became involved with a snowdrift, like your niece. I had some notion of sitting here, Liz, and trying to work out some solution to the murder of Fenwick Balderston, for which, as you may or may not know, the police of Dalton are most assiduously hunting me."

"Oh, Bill! I heard Frigid's Frozen News running on about the murder, but I never suspected that you—oh, you can be as bland and flippant as you choose, but you *are* in the hell of a mess! What happened? *Tell* me!"

"I wonder," Leonidas said, "if telling you might not be a tremendous help to me—but are you really sure you *want* to hear? And what about your niece? Suppose that she arrives and can't find you?"

"If she comes and can't find me, *she* can do some waiting for a change, herself!" Liz returned. "Go on, Bill, tell me!"

"Niece," Leonidas said thoughtfully. "Niece—Liz, I distinctly recall that you were an only child!"

"Oh, she's *George's* niece—get *on, tell* me!"

Leonidas wondered if he could ever inveigle her into

159

mentioning George's last name, or George's business, or George's whereabouts, or George's status.

"Well, after escaping with Harriman and your package —and just one thing more before I embark on this recital, Liz. Er—*why?*"

"You certainly ought to know the whys of this mess better than I!"

"I mean, *why* the dinosaur's footprint? Not only do I yearn to know myself, but I faithfully promised a young friend of mine that if I could find out what the thing was, I would also discover just why anyone would want it— er—*why*, Liz?"

"I've been so hoping," she said, "you'd forget to ask that! It's so *silly!* I have a friend, Ruth Basham, and we just send each other silly things—it's the sort of nonsense that's such fun, and sounds so thoroughly foolish when you tell about it. Her last gift to me, for example, was a large chunk of the Great Wall of China. And when I read in the *Dalton Chronicle* this afternoon that a dinosaur's footprint was among the articles to be sold at an auction in Pomfret, *nat*urally I rushed over to get it at once! I practically broke both legs getting there! I mean, *can* you think of a finer answer to a chunk of the Great Wall of China than a dinosaur's footprint?"

"Frankly, no," Leonidas said. "You make it sound very, very logical, and it only makes me wonder all the more why and how in the world Emily Pushing had the wit to make such a purchase!"

"First," Liz said judicially, "I just think she nodded her head at the wrong moment—you know how that happens at auctions! And then I think she was sort of *pleased* with herself. After all, a dinosaur's footprint isn't something that every Tom, Dick or Harry *has* kicking about his house! That's another reason I wanted it for Ruth, incidentally. She's such an awfully hard person to get things for anyway. She *has* so much!"

"M'yes," Leonidas said, "it's unquestionably the ideal choice of a gift for the person who *has* everything! And how amazing that no museum had a representative there to bid for it—or is it merely a dinosaur's footprint by hearsay, or acclaim, or general consent?"

"Emily said two museum men were there, but this wasn't large enough to suit them," Liz answered. "I don't know whether this piece is just the print of a baby dinosaur, or only part of a paw-print or hoofprint, or whatever dinosaurs printed with when they walked. But it was found years ago on some farm in Pomfret, and is highly authenticated—it has practically a pedigree!"

"Er—you mean, 'This print is from the left rear foot of Oth, third son of Goth and Moth—' "

"I mean there are letters from Harvard and the Smithsonian and all, saying that they've examined it and investigated it, and that it's the genuine print of a genuine dinosaur! I stuck the papers in my pocketbook, or you'd have found the whole history in the package—don't you really think it'll make a nice flagstone for a terrace border, or a nice sundial top?" she added irrelevantly.

"Oh, definitely, definitely! Marvelous to set hot teapots on, too," Leonidas said, "and if one lost the—er—pedigree, one could always frame it as a relic of the London Blitz."

"Well, I keep thinking if I used the Great Wall of China, Ruth can certainly figure out some good way of using a dinosaur's footprint!"

"And just what was your—er—modus operandi, may I ask?"

"I had that chunk inserted in the top front step of my new house."

"A conversation piece?" Leonidas inquired.

"Not particularly, just using it as the Chinese did," Liz said. "An optimistic barricade against intruders. Now, Bill, stop frittering time away, and *tell* me what happened!"

"After my escape in Harriman's coupé, huddled on the floor of the car and clutching your package to my bosom, I went to Balderston Hall, where I was to dine with Fenwick—"

Step by step, he went through the whole story—from the little bust of Shakespeare that had been used as a murder weapon, and Thor and Inga in the wine closet, and the table set for another dinner guest, and Doctor Fell's arrival with the Roquefort cheese, and his own precipitate flight, to his rescue by Shaver and their retreat to Carnavon. He touched on Shaver's disclosure of Fenwick's little milliners, and noted the brief presence in Fenwick's front hall of the monkey who was eating a Delicious apple, and the quart of ice cream, and the mink coat.

"And don't interrupt, Liz, and ask me, because *I* don't know what happened to them any more than Shaver did! They simply disappeared during the brief interval he was in Fenwick's library!"

"I wasn't going to ask what *became* of them, Bill, but what *flavor*—"

"I feel in my heart that it could only have been pista-

162

chio. Then Shaver and I advanced to the Carnavon branch of Devlin's Thirty-one Flavors, and at the exact moment when I discovered that the little brown paper package's label bore Emily Pushing's name, Emily and Yeoville marched over the threshold—"

"And I know *why*, too! At this point, I know every wearisome detail of their prosaic lives!" Liz said. "They'd promised someone to get some soda straws for the club —no one ever explained what the straws were *for*—and they combined a duty visit to Yeoville's aged mother in Carnavon with the errand. Yeoville simply *adores* magicians, I may add, and certainly wasn't going to let a few flakes of snow keep him from seeing this Blinko chap, ha ha ha! And if Yeoville said once that the hand was quicker than the eye, Bill, he said it some twenty thousand times! Go on—I don't mean to keep interrupting so! Then what?"

He told her how Red had saved him from the police at Devlin's and of his interlude in the Ladies Lounge, of the trip to McLean's in Kilroy's sedan, and how Kilroy's good deed had been rewarded by the staving off of the Carnavon police on the homeward trek, and how finally he had opened the little brown paper package in order to satisfy Red's burning curiosity.

"Oh, I *like* this redheaded child!" Liz broke in. "What's she like? What's she look like?"

Leonidas told her.

"In short," he concluded, "she's practically Lilith in looks, and in the average modern novel or modern gutty murder story, she'd have the whole cast of characters swarming in and out of her bed. Actually, in spite of her

163

appearance, she seems to possess most of the prudent solicitude of a nice mother hen. I shan't be at all surprised to find that her hobby is knitting socks."

"Don't sound as if you were so disappointed in her, Bill!" Liz said with a laugh. "It's always been my experience that a good Amber character is actually plain as mud. Think it over carefully when you have more time to ponder! Why did you come back to Dalton? The fascination of sticking your head into the lion's mouth?"

"We decided that Fell would probably be staying at the Dalton Inn, and Red took on herself the job of luring him out—"

"I'm sure it wouldn't tax her at all!" Liz interrupted. "Child's play! I can see him marching out now, panting slightly! Even drooling."

"I wish," Leonidas said wistfully, "that I could share that vision!"

"Don't tell me that the child let you down!"

"She and Kilroy went inside," Leonidas said. "I sat in the sedan quietly reciting 'Thanatopsis' to myself, and then—then I made the fatal error of tempting the old octopus of fate too far! I saw Fenwick's new secretary, a beautiful blonde whom Shaver had told me about, starting to go into the Inn. And all at once, I decided she was the one who had left behind the pocketbook I mentioned finding back in Fenwick's library chair. So I got out—"

"But, Bill, you told me that when you and Shaver looked at that pocketbook in Devlin's, it was *ut*terly devoid of clews! What suddenly led you to believe that it belonged to this new secretary?"

"The clasp on the little green pocketbook was a large,

modernistic chromium beetle—did I omit telling you that?"

"You never even said it was green!"

"And the buttons on this girl's green topcoat were exact duplicates—absolutely identical beetles. And even in that light, I knew that the green of her topcoat matched the pocketbook. And I knew from Mrs. Mullet's description that she was also the girl who'd originally left the bank report at my house. So I rushed after her. And she at once screamed out in terror, as if I were some loathesome, repellent monster—and at once Sergeant Mac-Cobble appeared, and once again I went dashing—no, skating," Leonidas corrected himself, "skating is a better word. I went skating off into the night to be rescued once again by the invaluable Harriman, who'd been leaving Blinko at the Inn."

"A modernistic beetle—I suppose," Liz said reflectively, "that little green pocketbook is really an important clew, isn't it?"

"It's a clew, certainly—by the way, it's on the bench beyond you," Leonidas said, "if you'd like to see it. Of course," he continued as she picked it up and took it over to the window, "I had rather hoped that you could describe the girl you saw leaving my house as a beautiful blonde, wearing a green tweed suit with round silver buttons, and a green topcoat with beetle buttons. My pleasure would also have known no bounds if you'd been able to add that she flew away in a convertible beachwagon. Then the cycle would have been complete—first she brought the bank report, then she later stole it. Now, I find myself wondering—"

"Bill!" Liz's voice was suddenly very serious. "Bill, this isn't *good!*"

"No," Leonidas agreed, "when summed up in its entirety, I must admit that my story lacks quite a lot. While there is an apparent wealth of detail, there is at the same time an amazing paucity of detail that matters. But by establishing the person who stole my bank report as a girl, I wonder—m'yes, Liz, I think that you've rendered me a great service. I wonder—"

"I met Fenwick Balderston at the bank the other day, Bill. Only in a business way, of course—but he really *is* an important character around here, isn't he?"

"M'yes, he is indeed. Now, Liz, if this girl brought the bank report and later stole it, that very clearly indicates to me—"

"You haven't a whit of proof that it *is* the same girl, Bill!" Liz said impatiently. "Now, listen to me! This is a perfectly frightful mess for you, or for anyone to be in! *Fr*ightful!"

"Oh, I'm entirely reconciled to whatever happens to me!"

Leonidas was puzzled by the change which had taken place in his companion's attitude. Her tones had been gay enough when they'd been japing about the dinosaur's footprint, and amused enough when he'd been telling her of his various adventures. But now she sounded strangely solemn and strangely worried.

"What I *do* brood about, and with intensity," he went on, "is the fate of Meredith's Academy—did Emily Pushing volunteer the information that I own Meredith's? And there are fifty acres of land I absolutely *must* wangle from the woman who's bought Fairlawns, the adjoining estate—a feat I shall certainly never accomplish as long as the aura of suspected murder clings to my name! Actually, Liz, those acres are the real reason for my attempting to get to the root of this Balderston business! Only if I solve Fenwick's murder will I have *any* chance of inveigling her into giving us that land for our new buildings, without which Meredith's will not survive!"

"Oh," Liz said. "Oh."

"So solving this is my only course—m'yes, Liz, even your knowing that a girl left my house puts a new light on things. It's enabled me to have my first genuinely constructive idea. Now," he said briskly, "I certainly can't stay here waiting for Harriman very much longer. Could I—may I ask you to do something for me?"

She hesitated. "What, Bill?"

"Would you be willing to go back into the club and phone the Dalton Inn and ask for Doctor Fell? If he's there, pretend you wanted a Doctor Pell, and hang up. If he's out, I can still hope that Red and Kilroy have him, and that I can somehow locate them. I'll give Harriman a few minutes more—"

"*How* can you locate that pair, Bill? How can you get away from here?"

"If Fell is not at the Inn," Leonidas said, "I'll get away from here if I have to steal a pair of skis or break out the new snow plough. You can't guess what those fifty acres mean to Meredith's, Liz!"

"D'you know the name of this blonde secretary?" she asked suddenly.

"She's a Miss Cowe—with an 'e,'" Leonidas said. "Er— will you make that call?"

She drew a long breath. "Yes. Now, as I heard Harri-

167

man say to you, *will* you be careful, Bill, and stay out of more crazy trouble?"

"The only fatal calamity I can imagine occurring," Leonidas said, "would be to have Emily and Yeoville drop in. I like to think that by now they are both snug in their little beds—why were they waiting here, anyway? Were they stuck?"

"Yes, some man was bringing chains for their car. Bill," she paused in the doorway, "if you do run into any problems, I think you *might* pretend to be Blinko—if you keep your face out of the light! Oh, and he had an accent, by the way."

"Any particular species of accent?"

"A very hybrid sort of 'zeese' and 'zoze,'" Liz said. "Purely professional, I suspect. He's probably a Connecticut Yankee. And he referred to himself in the third person. Please be careful until I get back!"

"Your feet!" Leonidas said. "How thoughtless of me—could I lend you my borrowed overshoes?"

"Thanks, but I swiped a pair in the hall. Bill, are you *sure* it was Cowe, with an 'e'?"

"Positive. Why? Do you—"

But Liz had already gone.

Leonidas watched her trudge through the snow back to the club, her long skirts gathered up over one arm.

Something, he thought, had unquestionably happened after she looked at that little green pocketbook.

Did she recognize it? Did she know to whom it belonged?

Was it—could it be *hers?*

Could she—no, that was too utterly absurd! Liz Copley could never be anyone's little milliner!

But she certainly had proffered no details about herself. She had never mentioned George, except in reference to his niece. She had never given any reason for her being in Dalton.

And now that he thought of it, how quickly she had slipped over that long, low sedan, the Atomic Age vehicle! While she claimed to loathe it, she had made no attempt to explain why she drove around in it, or why she had those two uniformed giants who came running at the shrill piping of her whistle!

And she had of course been wearing a mink coat, back there on Birch Hill Road.

"If she's a milliner," Leonidas murmured to himself, "she is definitely a very successful milliner!"

Minutes passed.

On sudden impulse, Leonidas left the window and went over to the wooden bench.

Not only was the dinosaur's footprint gone—but the little green pocketbook was gone, too!

Had Liz found out all she wanted to know, and departed for good and all?

"M'yes," Leonidas said, "I rather suspect so!"

He belted Kilroy's coat, turned up the collar, and went to the door.

He would go to the telephone and find out about Doctor Fell, himself! He should have taken the chance in the first place. After all, he knew the club well enough to get in a back way, without being seen!

But the instant he slipped into the shadows of the east porch, he was accosted.

"Yoo-hoo!" A woman came hurrying over to him. "Yoohoo, Blinko, I simply *must* tell you how terribly much I enjoyed your—oh, it isn't Blinko, is it? It's Shakespeare! I mean, Mr.—oh, dear, I never *can* remember your real name, ever! My son always just called you Bill Shakespeare, you know!"

"M'yes," Leonidas said courteously, "and how *is* he?"

It was both a foolproof and an infallible answer which he had adopted after dealing with the mothers of countless generations of Meredith boys.

"Oh, Charles is simply doing marvelously! Magnificently! He has *two* routes, now!"

"Oh, indeed!" Leonidas said, wondering whether she meant two airline routes or two asparagus roots. "Indeed! How splendid!"

"His father's *so* proud! They're the two longest routes in Dalton, but of course Charles can manage them so nicely with Gustav and the car!"

Not the mother of a Meredith boy, Leonidas suddenly realized, but the mother of his former paper boy who had come in the Cadillac town car!

"Ah, yes!" he said. "M'yes, so he has new routes! I thought I'd missed his—er—touch lately!"

"*Every*body has, on his old route. Gustav taught him to be so terribly careful, you know—and so neat! The papers always folded just so, and always in the same place every time, and not up in gutters, or back among the evergreens, or out in the slush and wet! People are simply *mad* about Charles in Dalton Hills and around here by the club! You actually wouldn't believe how many ecstatic calls I've had about him!"

"Now I do hope," Leonidas said sincerely, "that you will congratulate his father for me—and I'm sure that you, too, have played no small part in his fine success!"

"Oh, I've lost eighteen pounds!" she said happily. "It's that horrid getting up in the mornings, you know! But my doctor's simply delighted about it—he'd tried to make me lose eighteen pounds for years and years—oh, there's Gustav, now! So awfully nice seeing you!"

She fluttered away, and Leonidas turned to continue on to one of the club's rear doors.

"Bill!"

It was Liz, apparently springing from nowhere, and desperately grabbing at his arm.

"Bill, is there any place inside where we can talk safely?"

"What's the matter?" Leonidas was shocked by the anguish in her voice. "What's wrong?"

"I don't know—but something's got to be done, and quickly! Where can we go?"

Leonidas led her to the nearest door, which opened into the club's darkened dining room, and unlocked it with his gold-plated key.

"Follow me carefully, Liz. Don't bump into any of these piled-up tables!"

He picked his way across the room, unlocked the door of a service pantry where the silver was kept, motioned her inside, and shut the door after them.

"Now," he turned the inside lock, "if we're quite quiet —what's wrong, Liz? Where did you come from so suddenly? What's the matter?"

"From the parking space. Bill, I know you've guessed about June—"

"June, as June the month?" Leonidas asked in honest bewilderment as she paused.

"June, my niece! June *Cowe!*"

"What?"

"Oh, I kept trying to tell you that if that little green pocketbook of hers was such an important clew, and this was such an important case, it was too awful and too frightful for you to cope with alone, and we'd better call my lawyers at once—but you just never gave me any chance to get it all out! And besides, I kept thinking it was all some perfectly horrible mistake anyway, even though God knows the thought flashed through my mind when that girl rushed from your house that she *looked* rather like June! And I *did* see a convertible beachwagon streaking away from near Emily's, just before *you* came bursting on the scene! But I thought if I could only lay hands on June, I could straighten everything out—she's always losing pocketbooks and strewing them around—"

She stopped from sheer lack of breath.

"Your niece!" Leonidas said. "M'yes, of course, if I'd had an iota of wit—"

"*Had*n't you guessed?" Liz demanded. "But you kept saying in an insinuating fashion that *my* having seen this girl had helped you so, and you knew her name! Naturally I thought most of your haste to get away was largely to snatch the child and turn her over to the police!"

"*I* was only trying to say that if someone had left the bank report and then taken it, obviously it was *not* a bank report at all, and that the wrong thing had been left at my house. And since Doctor Fell was so obviously—but let us not involve ourselves with all that ratiocination, now! What's the matter with June?"

"I don't *know!*" Liz said unhappily. "She's here—her beachwagon's down in the parking space, plenty of people have seen her, and she's been asking around for me. But—she's *gone!*"

"Er—*gone?*"

"I can't *find* her!"

"Oh, I'm sure she's about somewhere!" Leonidas said soothingly. "Did you try the—er—Ladies Lounge?"

"I've hunted this damn club from attic to cellar," Liz said in despair, "and I tell you, June's disappeared!"

"I CAN'T BELIEVE," Leonidas said slowly, "that—"

"But you can't finish that sentence, *can* you?" Liz returned. "*I* know! *I* can't believe anything awful's happened to her, either. I won't let myself. All I know is that she came here half an hour ago, people saw her, her car's here, but she isn't—I've gone all over this place, and she's just *not* here! Nor do I for one moment think she may be out desperately trying to get an eagle three on that long dogleg! Bill, where *is* she? Something's happened, and you know it! And we've got to find her!"

"Suppose," Leonidas said, "she thought that the package she brought to my house was a bank report, later discovered that it was not, and—er—whimsically, shall we say, chose to sneak in and snatch it when the truth dawned on her. That leaves her in possession of the thing, whatever it is, and consequently—" He broke off. Perhaps this was not quite the ideal time to suggest the possibility of consequent peril. "Liz, why in the world didn't you tell me that your niece worked for Fenwick Balderston?"

"I didn't know she did!"

"Er—you mean she's in the habit of working and not telling you about her job?"

"Yes—I mean, no! Oh, we haven't time to go into it all now, Bill! Her—well, let's call them guardians! Her

174

guardians have certain ideas, and her *not* working is one of them. She and I both, through no fault of ours, are in rather an awkward position about certain things. Like that horrid car of mine. She—no, she didn't tell me! She's tried working before, was always forced to stop, and I assume," Liz said, "she decided to try again, and felt that her chances of keeping the job were better if *no* one knew! She simply told me she was going to help out at the Friendly Aid for a while, purely for fun. How she got a job from Balderston, I can't—oh, yes, I *can* guess how! But we've no time for any such discussions! The point is, we've got to find June! Where *is* she? What can we *do?*"

"Are vast throngs still milling about?"

"Not throngs, but quite a few. Including, I hate to have to tell you, Emily and Yeoville."

"Whose presence alone," Leonidas said, "constitutes a titanic handicap. Counterbalancing those two—er—ill-winds, however, I have a key which will open any door in the place. Did Blinko have props? Rabbits, perhaps?"

"A rabbit. He gave it to some woman in the audience, to Yeoville's annoyance. He pined for it."

"Very well, I'm Blinko, hunting the other rabbit which escaped. It's a weak solution, but we've so little choice! Come on, Liz. If anyone appears to be about to accost Mr. Witherall, you leap to the fore and announce with élan that *Blinko* is hunting a lost rabbit. If you say it firmly enough—well, let us go!"

Fifteen minutes later, they had finished a fine-tooth combing of the club's first floor, including the kitchen, the ells, the locker rooms, and innumerable closets.

"Is your neck stiff from ducking?" Liz inquired as they mounted the back stairs to the second floor.

"That at least two dozen people have not spotted me," Leonidas said, "is a major miracle. And possibly a portent. Perhaps the old octopus of fate has chosen to smile on me again!"

They covered the second floor.

They went through the attic.

They descended to the cellar.

"You see," Liz said grimly after a minute inspection which had included the incinerator, the unused coal bins, and the boiler room, "you see what I mean? June isn't here! Bill, she must have been taken away! That must be the answer—and you must be right! I mean, in what you didn't break down and say. There's something to do with that package you think she took, and it's mixed up with this murder, and June's mixed up with it—and someone's kidnapped the child!"

"Any girl whose scream possesses her intensity and pitch," Leonidas returned with a confidence which he did not in the least feel, "was neither lured nor removed from this club without considerable earsplitting hullabaloo! Not if the mere sight of me could rouse her to such—er —clarion hieghts!"

"Where are we going now?"

"Back to do it all over again. We must have overlooked something," Leonidas said reflectively as they started up the stairs to the main floor. "Something new—for we've certainly covered every inch I know! I still can't believe— oh, but there must be some extraordinarily simple explanation, Liz! There are too many people around—"

"I dare say," Liz interrupted with crispness, "that Fenwick Balderston had servants, neighbors, and friends who could be summed up loosely as 'people around'—oh, duck! *Duck,* Bill! Pushings!"

They ducked into the dining room, and Leonidas hurriedly led the way back to the service pantry which they had so recently vacated.

"I'm sure they didn't spot us after all!" she said as Leonidas again turned the inside lock. "Just in the *nick* of time, that fat man spoke to Yeoville and they looked the other way!"

"But perhaps we'd better whisper, Liz, just in case any dark suspicion crossed their minds, and they take it into their respective heads to investigate! I'm convinced that there is some extraordinarily simple answer to June's disappearance!" Leonidas said. "But I can't think of any place we've not peered into or groped into, and she most assuredly cannot be in this pantry—but now I wonder! M'yes, I really wonder!"

A minute later, his hand found the dangling light cord, and jerked at it.

Thirty seconds later, they were surveying the trussed-up form of June Cowe, stuffed into the oversize laundry hamper a scant two feet beyond them.

"Sssh! Not a word, Liz!" Leonidas said quickly. "And before we remove her gag," he went on, looking into the blue eyes staring balefully at him from the hamper, "perhaps she should be warned that I am the man with the beard at whom she so vigorously screamed outside the Dalton Inn, and cautioned most forcefully against repeating the performance now!"

"But how could she have—"

"And advised," Leonidas continued, "that I am a kindly

177

old gentleman who is only doing his best—in short, no loud sounds, Miss Cowe! And no loud questions, Liz! She's obviously in the very best of health, and that is the most important factor! Perhaps we might very well refrain from any comments whatsoever until we are safely out of here and into her car—I am extremely uneasy about Emily and Yeoville!"

After untying the knotted napkins which served as her gag, and which had bound her wrists and ankles, they permitted her a brief moment in which to stretch, flex her cramped muscles, and work her jaw. Her mouth was creased where the tightly drawn gag had pinched into her skin, her cheeks were smeared with streaks of lipstick, and she was obviously stiff.

But whole! Leonidas thought thankfully.

He shepherded them out the dining room door, after assuring himself that the Pushings were not lurking in the vicinity, and the trio made their way down to the parking space.

Leonidas was not at all surprised to discover that he was once again clutching under his arm both the little green pocketbook and the little brown paper package containing the dinosaur's footprint. He had quite automatically picked them up from the pantry shelf where Liz had placed them while they were undoing June's bonds.

"Now," he said as they piled into the front seat of the convertible beachwagon, "I'm delighted to see that you are—er—intact, Miss Cowe, my name is Witherall, and —er—exactly *what* has been happening to you?"

"From what I could hear back in there," June said, "I gathered you already—wow, my jaw is stiff, and my

mouth tastes like a crumpled-up ball of old brown paper!
—I gathered that you already knew practically all. Except you can't possibly dream how violently I worked to
make a noise so you'd hear me, when you first came. I
know I made that hamper wiggle, but you didn't put the
light on and couldn't see it—and let me tell you that the
way my wrists and ankles were strapped together, every
small movement was so much torture on the rack! But
I'm sure you know as much of what's happened as I do,
if not more! And did I thank you? Because," her pleasant,
somewhat husky voice broke for just the fraction of a
second, "because it's so lovely being out here!"

"Darling, how did you get *into* that thing?" Liz demanded. "And are you really all right?"

"My head throbs—feel the lump? And I don't know.
Oh, Liz, I really should have told you about the bank! I
was a louse not to. I went there to cash a check, and met
Mr. Balderston, and touched him for a job, and got it—
oh, damn, I'd so hoped this would work out! Have you a
cigarette? I seem to have lost my case."

"The hamper, darling—how did you get *in?*"

"I told you, I don't know! One minute I was here by
the parking space, hunting for you—somebody said he
thought you'd come out to wait for me—and the next
minute, I was coming to darkly in that hamper. I didn't
even know it *was* a hamper. I don't know *who* hit me.
But someone did! Or what hit me—oh, it's curry!"

"Er—curry?" Although much of the tenseness had disappeared from June's voice as she continued to talk,
Leonidas suddenly found himself feeling a little perturbed about the girl. "*Curry?*"

"That napkin I've been biting. It tasted of curry—and

old brown paper. I just—Liz, darling, I think someone's picked my pockets! I haven't any cigarette case, or lighter, or matches, or gloves—what a mercy I left the keys here in the car! At least we have those! At least," June said as she opened the glove compartment, "I *hope* we do—oh, look! They're here, but everything's been messed around! Rifled! And the longer I sit on this seat, the surer I am that someone's had it out—yes, see? It's all out of place! Well, that's the answer. I seem to have been robbed and ransacked!"

"And where," Leonidas tried to sound casual, "was the bank report you took from my house? In your coat pocket, or here in the car?"

"Oh, that *thing!* That simply unspeakable *thing!*" June said with deep feeling. "Neither. I mean, I didn't have it."

"Er—where *is* it?"

"Don't I wish I knew!" June said, and gave a weary sigh. "What else d'you think I've been tracking like a bloodhound through snow storms and snow drifts and general travail?"

"Miss Cowe," Leonidas said patiently, "may we—"

"Look, I *have* seen you before somewhere, haven't I? I mean, before that little episode outside the Inn?"

"He looks like Shakespeare, darling," Liz said, "he always has, he cultivates it, he revels in it, and *do* call him Bill and get it over with!"

"Perhaps," Leonidas said, "the wise course is to achieve some solid basis by a chronological account of your first day in the bank as Fenwick's secretary, with particular emphasis on all data concerning that small brown paper-wrapped package which you left at my house. Er—you hung up your coat, you sat down at Miss Scaife's desk. What then?"

"It was really rather a frightful day, you know," June said honestly. "I did absolutely everything wrong except the letters—Mr. Balderston admitted that I turned out a devastatingly handsome letter, but I gathered that he also hoped for a number of other skills. Anyway, when I gave the errand boy the batch of directors' reports, I forgot to include yours, Mr. With—oh, it's really *hard* to think of you as Bill! You've been Witherall the Director, Witherall the Ogre, for so long!"

"M'yes, I see—and so you decided to bring the Ogre's report in person?" Leonidas asked.

"By the time I discovered I'd forgotten it, I was in a covering-up stage," June said. "Covering up Miss Cowe's moronic lapses was virtually my sole aim in life! I took the damned report to your house and gave it to a sort of stout Witch of Endor—I mean, she welcomed me charmingly, but her head was all done up in a dust cloth turban, and she was riding a broom. And that, I tell you with pain, is the crux of this hellish situation!"

"But, darling," Liz said plaintively, "I thought that it *wasn't* a bank report you took to Bill's house!"

"When I left it there, *I* thought it *was*—you've got to keep my delayed reactions straight, Liz! Then I went to Mr. Balderston's house to deliver a special delivery letter that came after he left, and that I thought might be important. It wasn't, of course, but he was obviously terribly pleased to see me in there pitching so hard. He patted me on the back in a kindly fashion and allowed that I was catching on very nicely. I glowed with pride! I glowed with pride half the way home. And then I suddenly remembered the labels! You see, at one point during the early afternoon, I'd typed off two labels. One for your forgotten report, Bill, and the other saying 'Mr. Balderston—Personal,' for a package of his."

"Eureka!" Leonidas said simply, as she paused to light another cigarette. "Now, tell me—exactly what did this package contain?"

"I honestly haven't the remotest idea, Bill!" June said. "It was all done up when he gave it to me and told me to label it 'Mr. Balderston—Personal.' I thought at the time it was probably one of those reports for his own personal use, because it was about the same size and shape—but for all I know, it could have been a dozen pairs of gossamer stockings for his best girl, or—"

"The little milliner!" Liz exclaimed in triumph. "I *knew* she'd come into this! I felt it in my—"

"Er—please!" Leonidas said. "Let us not digress from this label situation. You had two similar packages, one containing my report, the other containing some personal property of Fenwick's. Then what occurred?"

He felt it would be hoping too much to have her admit directly that she had mixed the labels, and he was not disappointed.

"The only other human being in that bank who's under ninety-six," June said, "is a very likely looking lad with glasses. This rare contemporary figure was passing by my door, and I leaned on my pickaxe, so to speak, long enough to take a look at him. Then—"

"You must ask him to dinner, darling," Liz said. "Bill thinks Shaver's very amusing. Did he make a face and mix you up with the labels?"

"He utterly ignored me, if you must know! Then Mr. Balderston buzzed, and I did eight or ten other little things, and then I went back and gaily labelled the packages. And not until I was half way home did it dawn on me that I'd put the wrong label on the wrong package! I hadn't thought of it before. I don't know why I thought of it then. But all of a sudden, I simply *knew!*"

"Oh, darling, I know!" Liz said sympathetically. "It's like the salt. When I was first married to your uncle, I used to find myself standing stock still in the kitchen, knowing I'd put the salt in something twice. And there you *were!*"

"Exactly!" June said. "There I *was!* Well, I turned around and drove back to Birch Hill Road. Mr. Balderston hadn't actually said his package was important, but I felt it probably was, and I simply *hated* to have to confess making such an idiotic mistake—particularly after he'd been so sweet and patient and forbearing. I kept wishing I could just slip into Bill's and get the package from the Witch of Endor, take it to Balderston Hall, and have that sweet little butler exchange it for the other! Then I could take *that* back to Bill's! I mean, it was absolutely an *ideal* solution—"

"Which no one, darling," Liz said, "except one of your years could possibly conceive of as going off without hundreds of hitches and muddles!"

"But there was such a *won*derful chance that neither of them had opened their packages, Liz! Mr. Balderston's was lying unopened on his desk in the library when I was there! I *saw* it!"

"Several Eurekas," Leonidas said. "And so you attacked

my house from the rear in the hope of contacting Mrs. Mullet—and found my back door open? Or the garage door leading into the back hall?"

"The garage door. But first I peeked into your window, and saw your package—lying unopened on a table by a door!"

"My local reputation for eccentricity," Leonidas remarked, "will surely be enhanced after this evening's group of—er—peering females! So you sneaked in by the garage door and took my package—after first nearly tripping over an electric cord in the hall? M'yes!"

"And then I heard you running down the stairs!" June said. "So I sneaked into a sort of cupboard thing under the stairs and crouched there—frankly, I don't think I suffered as much in the hamper! I mean, it was *aw*ful! Then when I heard you go toward the back of the house, I cut and ran out your front door. I couldn't have *borne* it all another single second!"

"Liz," Leonidas said, "briefly sum up your own position at that moment for her benefit!"

Liz obliged, with gusto.

"Now," Leonidas finally put an end to their involved computations of how Liz must have arrived after June had entered the house, and of exactly where the other had been at which time, "now, back to the package. After fleeing from my house in this car, which you had left below Pushing's corner, you took the package back to Balderston's?"

"Well," June said hesitantly, "well—this is going to sound so silly to you! Perhaps I took it there, and perhaps I didn't. I don't know. You see, I lost the damn thing!"

"Where?" Liz and Leonidas demanded in unison.

"I told you, I don't know where it is! Or where I lost it, or when I lost it! I've been trying to *find* it! When I got out of this car in front of Balderston Hall," June said, "no package!"

"But darling, it must just have slipped behind the seat—"

"I pulled this car apart, Liz! Then I squared my shoulders and went in to tell Mr. Balderston the whole bitter tale—and found him lying there dead! I—oh, I don't know what happened to me!" June said with a shiver. "I just took to my heels! Somehow the only thing in the world that mattered to me was finding that package! Because, don't you see, if I had to tell the police what I'd been doing, and then I *had*n't any package—"

"You should have come straight home," Liz said, "and told me all about everything, at once! You poor thing!"

June reminded her tartly that it wouldn't have done much good.

"Because *you* were over on Bill's street, weren't you? Or just leaving, or just having left? Anyway, you weren't home!"

"But I was—at least briefly! I went back there to change—"

"Perhaps it would have been better if you'd taken longer to find that pump, Liz," June interrupted. "Perhaps we'd have met, then! Because I went right from Balderston Hall to Birch Hill Road to see if I could have dropped the package somewhere between Bill's house and where the car was parked, even though I was positive I'd put it on the seat beside me! But that whole neighborhood was in the most frightful state of confusion — more cops and dogs and people milling all around! So I couldn't even try—I'm sure," she broke off in exasperation, "*I* can't see anything to laugh at! What's the matter with you two?"

"All that confusion," Leonidas explained, "was caused by your aunt's pursuing me with a posse for stealing her dinosaur's footprint—but let us pass over that, for the nonce! What did you do then, June?"

"I drove around and around, but I never could get a real chance to hunt—that street is the most highly populated spot! Then I went back to Balderston Hall—oh, I stopped at a place on the way to get some food and coffee. I needed it! And Balderston Hall was alive with cops swarming all over. So I drove around some more, hoping that some time or other, they'd all go away long enough to give me another chance to hunt around by the gate, where I'd parked—and then it started to snow!"

"Darling, you should have come *home!*"

"But I knew you were at this thing at the club—didn't we spend hours last night figuring out what time I should come to collect you? And besides, Liz, I hardly dared to face you! You didn't know a thing about my job at the bank," June sounded very contrite, "but you'd get all the blame. And what those—"

"Yes, I know!" Liz said quickly. "But you must promise to let me know at once if you ever get mixed up in anything remotely like this again! Darling, d'you realize you might as well have been *killed* as merely thrust into that hamper?"

"I've been realizing I could be killed," June returned with a touch of grimness in her voice, "ever since the Frozen News spoke of a man with a beard being wanted for Mr. Balderston's murder—and I realized that *he* was

186

the man who was following *me!* That was after it got really snowing, and if you want to know the brutal truth, Liz, I never was so scared in all my life! And I didn't know what to *do!* I didn't dare go to the police without having that package, and I didn't want to get mixed up with things *any*way, and I didn't want to have to tell you what a mess I was in—oh, I was *torn!*"

"A man with a *beard?*" Leonidas sounded fully as bewildered as he felt. "Following *you?*"

"Yes, I'd been having this uneasy feeling that a car behind was following me," June said. "Then when it started trying to ditch me and forced me into snow banks, I knew! After the last time, I headed for the Inn. I was going to phone Liz I didn't think I could make it up here, Bill—I'd decided that spending the night there would be the safest thing. Then as I started through the revolving doors, I heard someone say my name, and turned and saw *you*—a man with a beard—right be*side* me! That's why I screamed and ran inside. I naturally thought it must have been you all the time, don't you see?"

"M'yes—but did you actually *see* this person with the beard? See him face to face?"

"Not face to face in a close-up, thank God! But the first time he jammed me into a drift," June said, "he jumped out of his car and started coming toward me—and I certainly know a bearded man when I see one, even in a snowstorm! Somehow I managed to get clear and get going before he reached my door. If I hadn't done all that driving for the Red Cross, I never could have made it— or any of the rest of the driving I've done tonight! I haven't covered very much territory, but the car and I have aged roughly thirty years apiece!"

"What did his car look like?" Liz asked.

"Like all the rest of the snow-trimmed cars out tonight," June said. "He was always behind me, or at an angle off my rear fender—and the visibility was approximately zero most of the time, remember! It was just his headlights always reflecting in my side mirror that put me on to him. You didn't actually *see* cars at that point. Only their headlights."

"Bill," Liz said, "d'you suppose there *is* another man with a beard? D'you suppose it was he who stuffed her into that hamper? Can you make *any* head or tail out of all this?"

"M'yes, I think she's unquestionably been followed by someone who wanted Fenwick's lost package, and suspected she had it," Leonidas said, "and I do feel it was he who finally caught up with her here. M'yes. And doubtless removed all those things from her coat pockets in the hope that the affair would appear to the naked eye as a casual, minor, or personal robbery. But as for the beard—June, when you entered the Inn after screaming at me, did you happen to see Blinko, a magician, a man with a beard, who was dressed not unlike me—and who, I assume, would have been surrounded by a certain amount of professional paraphernalia?"

"Yes! He had a dozen red boxes lettered with his name, and the police came in and grabbed him in the lobby. I saw it all from the phone booth where I was trying to get the club. I couldn't understand what it was all about," June said. "I knew he wasn't *you*—or *my* man with a beard—and I didn't feel a bit safer after they led him away. But then I saw Mary Painter wandering around dejectedly with her arms full of car chains—she was trying to find some way of getting up here and helping her family get home, and her own car had just succumbed to a broken axle up the street. I decided I'd be safe enough with her along, so I brought her back up here with me. I never *could* get the club on the phone, by the way. Mary said she'd been able to earlier, but couldn't later. The line must be out of order."

"I discovered that, Bill," Liz said. "I really *did* try to get your Doctor Fell for you!"

"Oh," June said interestedly, "did *he* come? Do you know Doctor Fell, too, Bill?"

"Er—no," Leonidas returned. "Do *you*—I fervently hope?"

"Why, I feel as if Doctor B. J. Fell and I were old, dear friends!" June said. "Chicago Operator Fourteen and I spent practically the whole morning getting him on the phone for Mr. Balderston! D'you remember the poem? 'I do not love thee, Doctor Fell—' "

"In its entirety," Leonidas assured her. "I am also well acquainted with its Latin counterpart, *'Non amo te, Sabidi, nec possum dicere quare; Hoc tantum possum dicere, non amo te!'* What kind of doctor *is* he, June? And *who* is he? And why was Fenwick telephoning him? And why was he coming here to Dalton?"

"Do you know," June said, "you ask the damnedest things, Bill! Would you seriously expect me to ask my boss if he were calling his dentist or his vet, and was it *his* molar, or his dog's? He just told me to get a number, and I got it—after a certain amount of travail! But I do know that Fell expected to come right away by the next available plane. Oh, and he was bringing a Roquefort cheese—no, I wouldn't know why!" she added as Liz

189

started to interrupt. "I just caught those random details as I went into Mr. Balderston's office a moment before he hung—"

"June, quick! Start the car!" Liz said. "Quickly! Oh, *hurry!* I thought I saw the Pushings, and it *is!* Hurry up, June—let me handle this, Bill! Hello, Yeoville!" she called out airily. "Hello, Emily dear! *So* sorry we haven't room for you! Blinko lost his rabbit, and I've been helping him catch the poor little thing—such a lovely, lovely evening! Good night, darlings! And," she went on in an undertone, "if you get stuck or stopped within the next half mile, June Cowe, I'll stuff you back into that laundry hamper! Get out of here, quick!"

"Liz darling, I'm trying!" June said as Yeoville kept pace with the backing car, "but this snow is now *slush,* and I can't—"

"Good night, Yeoville!" Liz called again. "*So* nice—June, *git!*"

FIVE MINUTES LATER, after the most hair-raising drive Leonidas had ever taken, June slowed down.

"All right," she said sweetly. "I *got!* And now what would you like me to do? Home? Town? Where?"

"Town," Leonidas said. "The Dalton Inn, please. And while I'm—er—struck dumb with admiration at your dazzling exhibition of race-track driving through this incredible slush, don't you think it might be well if we arrive at our destination intact? And by the way, June, when you were at the Inn, d'you recall noticing a red-headed girl and a very large young man in the lobby?"

"I saw a terribly cute redhead. Every man in the place was goggle-eyed at her. She—"

"Bill," Liz interrupted unhappily, "this all just gets worse and worse, really! I mean it's *nice* that June could explain about those mixed-up packages, and *nice* to know that Balderston knew Doctor Fell, and all—but none of it *gets* us anywhere! You can't—*we* can't ever solve this! Much as I loathe the thought, we'll have to go home and call the lawyers and—"

"Er—no," Leonidas said. "No. As a matter of fact, I think that the situation is becoming progressively clearer. Crystal, practically. A certain definite element of cohesion begins to creep in. Consider, Liz. June left Fenwick's package at my house, later stole it, and lost it. And so, of course, now we know the motive for the murder!"

"Oh, *do* we?" Liz said with rising inflection.

"M'yes, someone killed poor Fenwick for the contents of that very package. So—"

"But how in the world do you know that? What makes you sound so terribly positive about it, Bill?"

"When June went to Balderston Hall with the special delivery letter for Fenwick, she noticed that the little brown paper package was on his library desk," Leonidas said. "But there was no such package—no bank report or reasonable facsimile—when I was there. The package was gone, and I think we may assume that the murderer took it—particularly in the light of what has since occurred to June. And I can just barely imagine his feelings," he added reflectively, "when he opened his little package and discovered that what he actually had was my bank report! How very, very disappointing for him! M'yes, indeed!"

"And so then he took to chasing me!" June said. "But why *me?* How could he possibly know about my mixing up the labels and the packages?"

"I very much doubt if he had any inkling of all that. I suppose he merely felt that Fenwick's secretary might be responsible for the error," Leonidas said. "It's a conclusion I should have arrived at in his place. Er—did you happen to mention your name while you were calling Doctor Fell, June?"

"No—yes! I did! I forgot and said 'Miss Cowe speaking' instead of 'Mr. Balderston's secretary speaking' after I finally got him. And things like that used to take twenty-five points off your score at the business school I went to, too!"

Things like that, Leonidas thought to himself, could take even more points off your score when it came to murders!

"When did you leave your green pocketbook at Fenwick's?" he asked. "On your special delivery trip?"

"Oh, so that's where I lost it! I thought I'd just forgotten to take it from the bank," June said. "I never even realized I didn't have it until I paid for my coffee at that lunch room place. I had to use the mad dollar from my compact."

"Bill, this bearded man bothers me so!" Liz said. "I suppose he's the murderer, isn't he? Now—does Doctor Fell have a beard, or has poor Blinko something to do with this, or is it someone *else* with a beard?"

"With Mr. Frigid flashing the news to the world that a man with a beard was being sought," Leonidas said, "a really intelligent murderer might well profit by the information, don't you think? If he put on a false beard, anything which he did while wearing it would, of course, be ascribed to me. In short, with a beard, he *was* me. If you will recall, June jumped to that conclusion at once." He paused to peer through the steamed window. "Are we really in the Centre? Your running time is infinitely better than Harriman's was several hours ago, June!"

"The slush is frightful," June said. "But there's a faint trace of some plough-work—where shall I park?"

"Around the corner from the main entrance, I think. And, Liz, will you go in and ask for Fell? I can't, and I feel it will be best if June parades herself as little as possible."

"Why, certainly, Bill! Only," Liz said plaintively,

"what'll I *say?* I mean, it's around half past one in the morning, you know, and just a bit late for the best people to go calling!"

"If Fell is there, improvise," Leonidas said. "Bring up Doctor Pell, the typographical error. If Fell is not there—and I suspect he won't be—leave a pleasant message from his aunt, and tell the desk clerk that this horrid storm delayed what was to be an evening call. And on your way in and on your way out, look for Red and Kilroy, or for any trace of them!"

"I don't know *why* you seem to keep feeling that they probably blazed directions for you on one of those lobby columns, Bill, or left a few strands of Red's hair draped over a rubber plant as a sort of mute beacon! And *how* I must look!" Liz said as June drew the car to the curb. "In these clumpy old gum boots, and my hair like a positive ball of twine, and my nose shining brightly—well, I'm off! I'll do my best!"

"It never occurs to that lambie-pie," June remarked as they watched Liz wade across the slush-choked gutter and a small adjoining lake, "that how her hair looks really matters so little in that sable coat! Bill, there's so much of this mess that I don't understand at all! How did you get mixed up in things? And when were you at Balderston Hall? And what was that about some posse pursuing you—and something else that sounded exactly like a dinosaur's footprint?"

"D'you know," Leonidas said thoughtfully, "while I appreciate how irritating it must be for you to have all these loose ends—er—waving in the air like so many question marks, I don't think that I could sum up the events of this night again—no, I really could not! Let it suffice to say that we have all been cruelly bandied about by the old octopus of fate, but that we have thus far survived is to me a clear indication that the capricious creature views us with favor. M'yes."

"That boy with the glasses," June said very casually after a long pause. "Shaver. Do you really know him, or was Liz just needling me?"

"M'yes. He also is involved in this affair."

"Oh? How? Where is he?"

"I'm sorry to say that I lost him," Leonidas told her, "between six hamburgs and a Ladies Lounge. But I prefer to think he is merely mislaid—ah! Here's Liz coming back!"

"I caught a glimpse of myself in a lobby mirror," Liz announced as she forded the gutter and wriggled into the front seat, "and I'm as revolting a sight—Fell's registered there, Bill. He left around eleven thirty, the clerk said, and hasn't come back yet. And look what was hanging on a branch of the very first rubber plant as you go in—*look!* June, light a match so he can see this sign!"

Leonidas put on his pince-nez and read the printing on the piece of paper she was triumphantly holding out to him.

" 'Kilroy,' " he said, " 'was here!' M'yes—and how very clever of them! They've got Fell! When they found me gone, they merely kept him, as I hoped. Now, I wonder— Birch Hill Road, please, June. Let us try my house. And approach slowly and with caution, because I should not be at all surprised to find that the Dalton police have left a—er—guard of welcome for me, despite the announcement of my arrest!"

"And what am I supposed to be if they're there?" Liz
195

wanted to know. "Your aunt from Brazil, where the nuts come from?"

"Brazil, Pennsylvania, perhaps, and delayed by this useful storm," Leonidas said. "Look for a note. And in the interests of personal safety, I think I shall take to the floor of this vehicle!"

As she started up Birch Hill Road a few minutes later, June reported to him that all seemed serene.

"No cars," Liz added, "and the Pushings haven't got home yet, either. No lights, and their garage doors are open—oh, yes, there *is* a cop outside your house! I can see him sitting on your doorstep! Well, I'll pump him."

Her conversation with Sergeant MacCobble, who apparently met her halfway up the flagstone walk, was clearly audible to Leonidas, huddled on the beachwagon's floor.

"Why, how do you *do*, officer! You're the one who was so terribly helpful earlier, when my little package was stolen, aren't you?"

"That's right, lady."

"And is Mr. Witherall home, do you know?"

"Mr. Witherall's been arrested, lady. He's in jail."

Leonidas's eyebrows rose.

"But he's my *cousin*, officer!" Liz said in shocked tones.

"I can't help that, lady. He's been arrested for a murder."

"A murder? Oh, there must be some perfectly frightful mistake!" Liz said. "Cousin Leonidas *could*n't do anything like that! Why, I never heard anything so utterly ridiculous! It's fantastic!"

"You wanted something here, lady?"

"My niece and I have been stuck for hours in this horrid storm," Liz said, "and we simply *can't* get home—we'd intended to stay here with him for the night. But under the circumstances, I suppose we'll have to go somewhere else—are you guarding the house?"

"That's right, lady."

"From curious sight-seers, I suppose, and all those morbid people who go around collecting odd souvenirs—have there been very many?"

"No, lady," Sergeant MacCobble said. "So far, only Kilroy was here!"

Liz's gay laughter trilled out.

"It's really not the sort of night when you'd expect many sight-seers to be out *except* Kilroy, is it? Well, I know there's been some simply fantastic mistake, officer! I can't believe anything like this of my Cousin Leonidas! Murder—why it's too ab*surd!* And if you see him, will you please tell him that his Cousin Liz was here, and to be sure and let her know if her attorneys can be of any assistance to him in all this perfectly awful nonsense? Thank you so much—good night!"

She returned to the beachwagon, which June proceeded to back around with some difficulty.

"*Why*, darling?" Liz inquired. "Why the hard way? I mean, why didn't you just keep going straight ahead instead of going through all this turning? This street just curves on itself—"

"After tonight," June said, "I know the curves of this vicinity as well as I know the lines on the palms of my hands! But as we swung around Pushing's corner, I thought I saw something, and I want to go back and look again. I'm not going to stop to gape, because that cop's standing there watching us, but I'm going very slowly, and you *see* if there isn't a sign or something pinned up on that corner lamppost! Try and make it out!"

"Er—*was* there?" Leonidas asked from the floor as the beachwagon again picked up speed.

"Yes, there was a sign," Liz said, "but it wasn't a message about Kilroy being there, or anything. Just figures, and I couldn't make them out at all—not at that distance and without my glasses!"

"A three," June said, "and a one—or maybe an eight and a one. Does it—"

"It does." Leonidas picked himself up and got back on the seat. "It most certainly does! They couldn't remain indefinitely outside the Inn, they couldn't stay here, so they pressed onward to Devlin's Thirty-one Flavors!"

"But there are millions of Thirty-one Flavor places!" June said.

"M'yes, but Red works in the one just over the Carnavon line," Leonidas said. "Er—can you bear the thought of bucking this awful slush that far, June?"

"It's actually getting easier all the time, Bill," she said. "If anything ever melted like magic, it's this snow! And at this point, I don't know that I wouldn't be willing to keep on to the South Pole or somewhere if only I could see everything all straightened out!"

"Bill," Liz said suddenly, "what's the matter with you? You're not half as pleased at tracking down Kilroy and Red and Fell as you should be! What's troubling you?"

"MacCobble," Leonidas said, "is causing me definite anguish. That man knows me, he knows perfectly well that I have not been arrested and that I am not in jail! I ask myself and ask myself, but I can find no conceivable

198

reason for his lounging on my doorstep in full sight of the world! Why is the excellent MacCobble choosing to display himself like some proverbial sore thumb? Why did he so very kindly inform you that Kilroy had been there?"

"Because I asked him, of course," Liz said, "if any people had been there! If he suspected anything, don't you think he'd have asked me questions, or asked June questions, or searched the car? D'you think he'd just touch his cap politely and let me go the way he did? Oh, police just aren't like that, Bill! You're crediting them with altogether too much subtlety! Will they be waiting inside Devlin's, do you imagine?"

"Er—I rather doubt," Leonidas answered, "if we'll find the trio sitting cosily at a table sampling the Bus Stopper's Special Quick Snack. But I do feel that something will happen the minute I show myself after we've entered the parking space there!"

The minute he did, Red popped out of a rear door of the restaurant, flew to him and hugged him, to the whistling envy of two passing truck drivers who witnessed the reunion.

"Oh, Mr. Witherall, gee, how wonderful to see you again! What I been *through!* Are you all right?" She hugged him happily again. "I never worried so much! And that Frigid Flash about how you'd been arrested— but we kept telling ourselves they'd only got Blinko, that magician that was in the Inn! And Kilroy's got Doctor Fell tied up in the back of the car!"

"Er—here?" Leonidas looked around the parking space.

"No, Kilroy comes here every half hour, and the rest of the time he's driving around all over seeing if he can't find you somewheres. He ought to be back again in about fifteen minutes—oh, Mr. Witherall, I'm so glad! And you got the notes all right?"

"M'yes, and rejoiced at your quick wit—"

"Oh, there's so much to tell you!" Red interrupted excitedly. "Kilroy knows all about Fell and who he is! He *did* know him, like he said!"

"Indeed? In the army?"

"No, he'd read about him in a magazine. Kilroy's been a great reader since he was out of the service. I didn't understand just what it was all about—you know how Kilroy talks! And besides, we been too busy. But it's sure made Kilroy take more interest in all this than I ever seen him take in anything for months. He—"

She broke off as the headlights of a car turning into the parking space suddenly caught them in its beams—and continued to spotlight them as the car braked to a noisy stop some three feet away.

Leonidas watched while Sergeant MacCobble got out from behind the wheel.

"Quick!" Red grabbed his arm. "Quick! The Ladies Lounge again! Come *on!*"

"Er—no," Leonidas said quietly. "It's no use. He knows. He followed us. I rather thought he would."

"But, Mr. Witherall—"

"Oh, Bill!" Liz appeared at his side with June. "Oh, what can we do! Whatever can we *do?*"

"Mr. Witherall, we *can't* let him get you now!" Red said unhappily. "Not after what we all been through to —say, what's he doing?"

Without paying the slightest bit of attention to the gaping quartet, Sergeant MacCobble walked slowly around his car, peering grimly at his tires as if he were subjecting them to some sort of visual third degree.

"The whole damn trouble," he said in a loud voice as he pettishly kicked at a front tire, "is my pension! I got to think of my pension!"

He stood back and surveyed the tire from a distance of several feet, an act which brought his shoulders so near Leonidas that they nearly brushed against the fuzz of Kilroy's coat.

But he never turned his head.

"How long we can get away with keeping this Blinko," the sergeant announced to the front tire, "I don't know! He plays a good game of gin rummy, and I told Artie to keep on letting him win."

"Er—the costs might be billed to me," Leonidas said casually.

"And to who else?" MacCobble asked the front tire. "Who *else*? Now I always said we never had a better Honorable President of the Police Widows and Orphans Benevolent and Protective Association than you was, back during the war. I haven't forgotten all them field days and dinners and all. Nobody ever got the dough rolling in like you. But I got my pension to think about, and when Blinko gets tired playing gin rummy with Artie, see—?"

"M'yes," Leonidas said. "I see. Er—how long, d'you think?"

"Not more than another hour. Two at most. Of course there's one thing," he said as ho kicked the tire again. "Nobody's going to bother you none because now you're caught. That ought to help you some."

"M'yes," Leonidas said. "Practically the Fifth Freedom. From Pursuit."

"You got anywhere, huh?" The sergeant almost forgot himself and turned around.

"M'yes, I think so. We know why he was killed, and that he had three other visitors besides myself and the murderer. And I know rather a lot about the murderer, but I've still things to clear up. Er—if I should happen to need your help?"

"I'll be hanging around your house. I had enough of trying to chase you for one night." MacCobble gave the tire a final kick and got back into his car. "Oh, sure, I been keeping tabs on you all right, but you'd always beaten it somewheres else by the time I got you figured out—the Ladies Lounge here, wasn't it? I decided that later. And then the triplets' birthday party. And—"

"Er—how," Leonidas inquired, "did you ferret out that one?"

"Oh, my brother Bill's a cop over here. He called and said the uncle of a guy helped him out of a drift was just a nice old fiddler, and not you. So we pieced it out. And then the Inn, and then the Country Club—uh-huh. I helped the chauffeur of that paper boy goes around in the town car's mother to get their bumper unlocked from a truck's. She asked me what did it mean when the Frigid News Flash said you'd been arrested, because she'd just talked with you at the club. I missed what Thirty-one was, but Kilroy—now that was good! And if you'd of *been* here," he added as he started the motor, "I'd of *seen* you, wouldn't I, when I was looking at them tires? You can't lose a pension for inspecting your tires! Two hours, mind!"

The car backed out of the parking space and roared off in the direction of Dalton.

"Now," Red said in awe, "I seen just about everything! Gee, he knows—and still he let you go!"

"Er—while MacCobble and I have locked horns in this sort of business on several previous occasions," Leonidas said reminiscently, "I must confess I never suspected that he had such implicit faith in my abilities! Nor am I entirely certain that this two-hour ultimatum may not perhaps prove more trying than pursuit might have been!"

"And all that nonsense you told him!" Liz said. "About having just a *few* things to clear up! Where's Kilroy? Where's Fell?"

"They ought to be back any minute now," Red said. "We got Fell tied up—gee, I can't help all the time thinking what poor Auntie's missing tonight! She—"

"Do forgive me for breaking in," Leonidas said, "but I must tell Liz and June that you are the niece of my good friend Mrs. Mullet—to whom you originally gave the package, June. And I'm thoroughly ashamed to admit, Liz, that I still cannot remember George's name!"

"I intend to call Red by her name," Liz returned cheerfully, "and I expect her to call me by mine. Are we just going to keep standing here while this slush whirls about our necks, or can we go inside and get something to eat? Now that I think of it, I'm simply ravenous!"

"You and June might go in," Leonidas said, "and perhaps bring out something for me when you return. Red and I will stay in the car and wait for Kilroy, because there may be some problems arising from the unleashing of Doctor Fell. Half a dozen hamburgs, I think, and some coffee."

"Gee," Red said after she and Leonidas had settled themselves in the beachwagon's front seat, "poor Auntie! And what a dream coat that Liz has on! Gee, I wish Auntie could see that coat—and she thought she was so big and important with this job she had tonight of monkey-sitting! Why—"

"Monkey-sitting?" Leonidas interrupted. "A job of *monkey*-sitting?"

"That's right. You know what baby-sitting is, Mr. Witherall. You sit with babies. Well, Auntie's got this friend that's a dog-sitter. She sits with dogs. She used to sit with babies, but dogs pay a lot better, and she likes sitting with dogs better, too."

"Er—why," Leonidas said, "sit with dogs anyway?"

"Well, there were these people in Pomfret Auntie's friend knew, see, and they had a dog that howled so bad every time they left it alone that the neighbors complained. So then they left on lights and the radio whenever they went out, but somehow that just made the dog chew the furniture legs, and he got splinters in his mouth, and howled, and the neighbors still complained. So they finally got this friend of Auntie's as a sitter for him, and now she's got about ten dogs she sits with regular. And—"

"But—er—*monkey*-sitting!" Leonidas persisted.

"I was getting to that, Mr. Witherall. Then she took up cat-sitting, and now she's got this monkey, too. But tonight she had a movie she wanted to see, so Auntie took over the monkey job for her." Red began to giggle. "And what do you think? If it cries, she has to feed it ice cream! *Think* of it! *Pistachio* ice cream!"

I NSTEAD OF JOINING in Red's gale of infectious laughter, Leonidas shook his head gravely.

"And the utterly appalling thing," he said almost to himself, "is that Mrs. Mullet actually started to tell me all about it before she left my house this afternoon! She tried, and you've tried to tell me once or twice—and I never let you! Now—you and your aunt live here in Carnavon, on Lubbock Street, do you not? M'yes. Well, perhaps you'd go in Devlin's and ask one of your colleagues to tell Kilroy to come to your house when he arrives. You and I are going to interview your aunt on the topic of this pistachio ice cream-eating monkey!"

"What about Liz and June? Shan't I get them?"

Leonidas considered for a moment.

"Point them out to your friend inside, and leave instructions for Kilroy to bring them along with him. We may as well permit them to finish their meal—and we don't really require their presence at this point. And time is marching on so inexorably!"

When she returned, Red hesitated at the beachwagon's door.

"Say, Mr. Witherall, could I drive? Gee, do I go for this type car!"

"M'yes, by all means." Leonidas moved away from the wheel. "You know the way—and I frankly find all that chromium gadgetry rather frightening."

"Say, who *are* those two? Gee, this is a *keen* job!" Red said as she backed expertly out of the parking space. "Where'd you pick 'em up? How'd you happen on 'em?"

He told her, briefly.

"So she's the one you snatched the package from, and the girl's the green pocketbook one. But who *is* this Liz, Mr. Witherall? With this swell car and that super coat— oh, if Auntie could only just touch a sable coat like that with the tip of her little finger, she'd die happy!"

In what seemed to Leonidas like the twinkling of an eye, Red drew up in front of a small, double frame house.

"And wouldn't I be driving home a car like this when the whole street's abed and asleep and can't see it!" she said. "Just my luck! Come along, Mr. Witherall, we live upstairs on this side."

His first view of Mrs. Mullet's spic-and-span living room gave Leonidas an uncomfortable feeling of ghostly reunion. Surely that was his old discarded Boston rocker in the corner? Yes, he recognized the design of gilt roses across the back. And that neatly upholstered green sofa— wasn't that the dishevelled thing which he had ordered out of his attic? And certainly that was his old wing chair which had spent so many years on its side in his cellar, its springs obscenely revealed among moldy glob-bets of felt!

"I guess you noticed your old radio," Red remarked. "Auntie told me you didn't think it could be fixed, but we get London on it fine. I'll wake her up."

She was back almost at once.

"Gee, she hasn't come home! She must of got stuck in the storm!"

"D'you know the address? Or the name of the monkey's owner?"

Red shook her head. "But Auntie said she'd leave the phone number in case I wanted to call her. *If* she did, and *if* we can find it!"

After what amounted to a practical ransacking of the apartment, Leonidas found a number written on a slip of paper that was sitting on the table a scant inch away from the telephone.

"And now," he said with a sigh, "for a bout with the Carnavon telephone book! I suppose we should exult and rejoice to think that Carnavon's population is one-tenth that of Dalton!"

Red found the listing a few minutes later while Leonidas was pausing to clean his pince-nez.

"Granby, Mrs. Elsie. Carnavon 1976. Business address —say, Mr. Witherall, I know who she is! She has a shop! A—"

"M'yes. A millinery shop?"

"How'd you guess? It's an awfully modern place with glass doors and indirect lighting and all. She has lingerie, too. I often look in the windows, but I never could afford to go inside. Summertimes, she closes up and goes to Magnolia, or Hyannis, or some resort place. And that home number's the Lancaster Arms—you know, it's that new place built around a lot of gardens over near the Carnavon Polo and Country Club."

"Leave a conspicuous note for Kilroy," Leonidas said, "informing him that he will find us there, at Mrs. Elsie Granby's."

Mrs. Mullet welcomed them with exclamations of excited pleasure at the door of Mrs. Granby's ground-floor

207

apartment, and led them through a little foyer into a living room.

As he entered, Leonidas received an overwhelming impression of fringe and ruffles and pale lampshades, of furniture that was just two sizes too large for the room, and of more pottery ash trays built to look like something else than he had ever seen before in one place in his life. His mind, groping for a descriptive word, hovered uncertainly between fussy and festooned.

"Isn't this a lovely room?" Mrs. Mullet demanded. "Such nice taste! And the monkey's been as good as gold! Never cried a bit, never once wanted his ice cream, just ate up his apple and went right straight to his bed like a good boy! See him there in the corner on his red blanket! Now—how'd you ever meet Red, Mr. Witherall, and *what's* all this I been hearing about you over the radio?"

"In Devlin's," Leonidas answered her questions in order, "and if you've been listening to Mr. Frigid, you doubtless know that I've been arrested for murdering Fenwick Balderston."

"In my candied opinion," Mrs. Mullet said indignantly, "those cops should all ought to have their heads examined! But I kept saying to myself it's all gist for his mill! It'll all help him with Haseltine! And do you know what's been driving me crazy? Come take a look in her boudoir here—this way!"

On Mrs. Granby's dressing table, amid innumerable jars and bottles and vials, stood a picture of Fenwick Balderston whose dimensions Leonidas guessed to be roughly a foot and a half square.

"Look at the gold in that frame!" Mrs. Mullet said with triumph. "Fourteen carat. I looked. I bet that cost a thousand dollars. I bet he's not just somebody she met yesterday while she was walking down to the A and P for a pound of coffee! No, Mr. Witherall, in my candied opinion, Mrs. Granby's known him pretty well for some time! And I kept saying to myself, if only I could tell Mr. Witherall about this! Honest, I bet I called your house every two minutes all the time Frigid's Frozen said you were being hunted—I only stopped when they announced they'd got you in custody! Because I know she was in Dalton around the time they said he was killed!"

"Indeed?"

"I came at six," Mrs. Mullet said, "and at six-thirty she told me she was breaking her dinner date and going to Dalton on a special important errand, something that'd just come up. She took the monkey with her. Then she came back around seven-thirty, with the monkey—"

"And a quart of ice cream packed in dry ice?"

"That's right! I don't know how you *do* it," Mrs. Mullet said rapturously. "Detecting a thing like that! Then she went out to this bridge party. She expected to be home by one, but I guess the snow hung her up like the radio said it did everyone. I—"

"Say!" Red interrupted. "Say, look, Mr. Witherall—there's a diary over there on her bedside table!"

"But it's locked," Mrs. Mullet said at once, with regret. "Don't you think, Mr. Witherall, that maybe we had ought to—"

"Er—no!" Leonidas said. "No, I most assuredly do not!"

"Neither do I."

The trio swung around.

In the doorway stood the woman who was obviously Mrs. Granby. She was blonde, she was plain-looking, she

209

wore a mink coat and a strange little hat of plastic roses, and she was—Leonidas found himself wondering. Fortyish? Or fiftyish? Probably Mrs. Mullet and Red could guess at a glance, but he couldn't tell how much was make-up.

Nor could he tell, from her immobile face, what she was thinking or what she was feeling. Nor had the tone of her voice given him any clew.

Nor had he any sense that she was assuming a pose.

Probably, he decided suddenly, she had used that look and employed those tones for years and years in her business. She was the buyer, waiting to be shown.

"Good evening, my name is Witherall," he said politely aloud. "I came with Mrs. Mullet's niece," his eyes never left her face, "to take her home. And to ask you quite candidly what you were doing this evening at Balderston Hall."

It seemed to him that she relaxed. Her hands, with their long scarlet nails, didn't fumble as she opened her pocketbook and drew out a cigarette case.

"The radio," she said, "announced that the police had arrested you."

"The radio erred. As a matter of fact, I rather expect to have the murderer within," he glanced at the tiny enamelled clock on her dressing table, "within an hour and twenty minutes. I should appreciate any help you might care to give me. Did you see that young man, Shaver, when he arrived?"

"Yes." She lighted a cigarette. "I'd gone in—the front door was open—and found Fenwick on the library floor. Then I heard someone coming, and ducked out into the hall, behind the stairs. Shaver came, and then I picked up Bappo and left. My car was parked at the garden gate. Shaver had nothing whatever to do with it. I'd gone to ask Fenwick's advice about a new store location I'd heard about late this afternoon—could I talk with you alone?"

Leonidas followed her into the living room. He had done right, he thought, to refrain from blustering, or accusing her. He had appeared to trust her, so she was going to help him. And he knew in an intuitive moment that if he had obviously mistrusted her, all the king's horses and all the king's men wouldn't have wrung one word from her.

"You're Leonidas Witherall, the one he called Shakespeare, aren't you?" she said. "Fenwick had great respect for your judgment. He said you knew less about banking than any human adult he'd ever encountered, but you never made a mistake in judgment. Mr. Witherall, what should I do? I know I ought to have stayed and called the police, but I couldn't! He was gone, and there was nothing I could do! It wouldn't have helped him to have Shaver find me there! I've been telling myself all evening that Fenwick understands. He was a business man. He'd be the first to understand what that situation would do to me! I haven't anything except my business. I couldn't stay!"

"M'yes," Leonidas said slowly, "I understand, and I'm sure Fenwick would. He was not sentimental about business. Mrs. Granby, have you any idea if Fenwick has lately acquired any object of great value? And I'm fully aware of the oddity of the question."

"It's odd you ask, because I've been thinking about just that. He phoned me this morning and said he'd just acquired something terrific in a very smart deal. He said now I could have a bracelet I'd wanted. I never married him," she added parenthetically. "He asked me to. But I wouldn't have fitted in with his friends, or he with mine. And that gloomy house he loved so! I'm not like him—"

She made a little gesture toward the room, and Leonidas, mentally contrasting the single bare bookshelf and the fringed furniture with Fenwick's library and Chippendale, found himself nodding. But he tactfully did not pursue the subject.

"You have no clew as to what this something terrific was?"

"I asked him at once, of course, but he only laughed and said that it was sitting on the desk in front of him in a brown paper-wrapped package, and that I wouldn't believe him if he told me what it was or what it was worth. That's all I know," Mrs. Granby stubbed out her cigarette, "although I certainly kept on trying my best to find out what the thing was!"

"Did you notice a little brown paper package on his desk in the library when you were at Balderston Hall?"

"No. But I saw that paperweight you'd given him—Mr. Witherall, why are you so sure I didn't kill him? Or are you only pretending?"

Leonidas smiled.

"You're very left-handed, as I've been noticing. You couldn't have killed him. I don't think you even could have gripped that paperweight without breaking one of your—er—long nails." He had only just escaped referring to them as talons. "Nor do you meet certain other specifications."

"But how do you know that the murderer was right-handed?"

"I have files at home," Leonidas said, "containing pages and pages of intricate and accurate reasons. My tendency is to forget the exact details between the periods during which I write books, but I will gladly send you all my data on the right-hand blow when I—er—have more time. Believe me that it was such! Mrs. Granby, you have definitely proved what I thought was true—"

He broke off as the apartment's door chimes played an intricate tune.

"At this hour, could it be—is it the police?" she asked nervously.

"No," Leonidas said, "I rather think it's a friend of mine. D'you mind if I go to the door?"

Kilroy stood beaming on the doorstep.

"Well, pal!" he said heartily. "Long time no see! I got Fell in the car okay. Want I should bring him in here, hey?"

"If you don't mind?" Leonidas turned to Mrs. Granby. "It has to do with Fenwick—m'yes, Kilroy," as she nodded, "bring him in. Only first, tell me—Red said that you know who Doctor Fell is?"

"That's right, pal," Kilroy said. "Listen, you remember when we was parked out in front of the Carnavon drug store, hey, and I said something about my having a dream, like?"

"M'yes." Leonidas wished in his heart that Kilroy might have chosen some less precious moment in which to enter into a discussion of his dream. But he had promised Red to find out, and he could do no less. "Something —er—about books, was it not? But you said that you did not wish to be a writer."

"No, pal, not that! See, it was all like this. In the army, they had a lot of books. I read some."

"Ah, splendid, splendid!" Leonidas said. "Admirable! Reading maketh a full man. Er—you want to *buy* a book, perhaps?"

"To *sell* 'em, pal! That's the story!"

"Er—you wish to own and run a bookstore?"

"Not like the kind they got around here, pal. The kind they have in London and Paris, see? Dirty little shops. Where you get—well, like treasures, see?"

"Er—you can't—er—d'you mean—first editions?"

After he realized that Kilroy did, and was in dead earnest, Leonidas removed his pince-nez in an effort to minimize and mitigate what he felt must be a very rude and very bewildered stare.

"That's right, pal! That's it! And leather bindings and all like that. What I want, see," Kilroy went on eagerly, "is to be like Fell, see? I read all about him in a magazine. He wasn't much, see. No college nor stuff like that —just like me, see? But he kept his eyes open, and now he trades in books—why, pal, sometimes that guy gets as much as fifteen grand for just one little book, like a magazine, see, that he found in some old ash can!"

"Er—'Tamerlane,'" Leonidas murmured quite automatically.

"That's right, pal! That's it! 'Tamerlane'! It's a pamphlet six and three-eighths inches by four and one-eighth inches," Kilroy seemed to be reciting a lesson, "with what they call 'tea-colored' wrappers. Only—say, pal, between friends, just what the hell *is* this 'Tamerlane,' hey? What's it all about?"

"It's a forty-page pamphlet, like a little book, or—or a

214

little catalogue—" Leonidas paused, put his pince-nez on again, and warmly shook the astonished Kilroy's hand. "Out of the mouths of babes and—er—m'yes, indeed. A little catalogue! But how exceedingly dull-witted I've been, Kilroy! Of *course* Doctor Fell was pawing around Fenwick's desk, looking for what seemed to me to be catalogues or pamphlets! M'yes, indeed! To be sure!"

"But what about this 'Tamerlane' job, hey?" Kilroy persisted. "What *is* it?"

"Omitting two lines from Cowper, the title page reads, 'Tamerlane—and Other Poems. By a Bostonian. Boston: Calvin F. S. Thomas, Printer. 1827.' The 'Bostonian,'" Leonidas said, "was actually Edgar Allan Poe, and if he had been anyone else, or if he had written nothing else, 'Tamerlane' wouldn't have mattered a whit. It's a very minor example of—shall we say—pre-bellum lyricism? I mean," he added hurriedly after a look at Kilroy's face, "it's rather mediocre verse. Er—"

"You mean it's punk poetry, pal?"

"Er—let us rather call it not very good. But because it was Poe's first published work, and because there are only seven or eight copies known to exist out of the some forty copies believed to have been printed by Mr. Thomas, it has grown to become practically the symbol of rare works in American literature."

"Say, pal, how do you know about all this type stuff, hey?"

"Oh, I've always collected books in a small, restrained way," Leonidas said. "I suppose I've hunted for a 'Tamerlane' in every bookstore and every junk shop I ever entered, in every book case I ever encountered, and in every attic chest. To find a 'Tamerlane' in some old bureau drawer, or to happen on one marked 'Ten Cents' is the dream of most book collectors, whether they admit it or not. My books at home are not very spectacular, Kilroy, but I'd enjoy showing them to you. Mrs. Granby," he turned to her, "the article which Fenwick described to you as 'something terrific' was undoubtedly a 'Tamerlane,' the pamphlet of which we've just been speaking."

"You mean, that's all that was in his little brown paper package?" she asked dubiously. "Just a little pamphlet?"

"Worth fifteen grand!" Kilroy said. "That's all!"

"M'yes, I'm sure a 'Tamerlane' is what Fenwick had," Leonidas said. "I'm also sure that he did it up himself with great care, doubtless protecting it with cardboard boards, and many, many layers of wrapping paper."

He paused and cleared his throat, and decided it would not be entirely tactful for him to suggest that Fenwick had been quite right in informing Mrs. Granby that she never would believe what his package contained, or how much it was worth.

"Fenwick's secretary," he continued, "said lightly that the package—which she erroneously labelled—might have contained a dozen pairs of filmy stockings. I dare say that the difference between it and my bank report with which it became confused was probably one of a few ounces in weight. And the dinosaur's footprint package, which I mistook for my bank report, was probably the heaviest of these three displaced packages. But all three were the same size and shape, and similarly wrapped in brown paper, and all were labelled with Dalton Bank labels. Now, Kilroy, can you manage to bring Fell in here unobtrusively, perhaps suggesting to any of the outside world who may be watching that you are merely assisting a drunken friend home?"

"Sure, but—well, pal, here's the problem," Kilroy said. "Fell's going to be plenty sore with me on account of what I gagged him and bound him up and all, and—I want to touch him for a job, see? You think maybe you can fix it up with him, pal? And what about the others? Should they come along in, too?"

"I'll try my best to—er—fix it," Leonidas said, "but I must admit to entertaining grave doubts. And m'yes, bring Liz and June in—if Mrs. Granby doesn't mind having a few more guests!"

"And what about that piano player, pal?" Kilroy inquired.

"Er—where did we acquire an accompanist, may I ask?"

"At Devlin's. He's a friend of June's, see? You ought to hear his 'Honeysuckle Rose,' pal! Strictly out of this world! Pure Fats Waller!"

"Indeed? A friend of June's? Er—" Leonidas began to smile. "Is he by chance wearing a dinner jacket, and glasses? A tall young man? M'yes! Do ask Shaver to join our little group, by all means!"

Shaver was grinning widely as he assisted Kilroy in bringing in Fell, who was bound and gagged as neatly as June had been.

"Oh, *vieux octopus du destin!*" he said. "They laughed when I sat down at the piano as those cops oozed into Thirty-one Flavors after you. But I'm happy to be able to tell you that I've made fifteen dollars and fourteen cents in small change that's been tossed at me, and the manager said cordially I could have a steady job there any time I wanted. Beats my little bank stipend—what d'you want us to do with this character?"

"Make Doctor Fell as comfortable as possible on the sofa, please," Leonidas said. "Liz, what *have* you got?"

"Hamburgs for you—you asked for them! And some terribly nice-looking cheese cake. Hi, Red, and of course you're Mrs. Mullet," she added as the latter came into the living room. "How do you do? And of course Mrs. Granby and I are practically old friends! My dear, I simply adore that awful stovepipe hat with the feathers, I practically haven't had it off my head!"

For a brief second, her eyes met Leonidas's, and said with triumph, "Little Milliner!"

"Mrs. Granby," she went on, "this is my niece, June Cowe. You'll have to do something about her hats. I can't ever tell whether she's wearing one or not—why, now that we're settled, there's practically everyone here but Emily and Yeoville, isn't there? Bill, what's gone on?"

"Fenwick's package contained a 'Tamerlane'—"

"Never! Oh, I've always longed to find two things—a 'Tamerlane' and a hunk of ambergris! What else have you found out?"

"Er—I'm getting to that. Doctor Fell," Leonidas thought he had never seen anything more vicious than the fury displayed in the doctor's little beady eyes, "I truly do regret the inconvenience which has been caused you by our somewhat informal and impromptu actions, and before you have any chance to exercise your constitutional right to protest loudly and hand us over to the police, I should like to make some effort to clarify the situation."

"Doctor Fell," Liz said, "is probably not the only person who would benefit by a bit of clarifying and you haven't forgotten that deadline, have you?"

"Miss Cowe, Fenwick's secretary," Leonidas went on imperturbably, "mislabelled the package containing his newly found 'Tamerlane,' brought it to my house in the belief that it was my bank report, later stole it in a—er —fit of consternation—this was her first day at work— and then, she lost it. The person who murdered Fenwick for 'Tamerlane' actually took my bank report instead. I trust that this is all quite clear to you?"

"I don't know how he does it!" Mrs. Mullet said in a hoarse, proud whisper.

"Neither," Liz said, "do I!"

"Now," Leonidas said, "let us briefly sum up the progress we've made in tracking down the murderer. We've learned quite a lot about Fenwick's visitors of the evening. Miss Cowe went there to deliver a letter, and left her pocketbook when she departed. Mrs. Granby, here, later arrived to discuss some business matters, and found Fenwick dead. She went just after the arrival of Shaver, over here, who works at Fenwick's bank. He came on the scene, viewed it, and departed. Miss Cowe popped back briefly—and then, I rather think, you came and left, Doctor Fell—although you possibly may have come just before Mrs. Granby. Then I arrived. Then you made your official entrance."

"Summed up in that bald fashion," Shaver said, "there's more than a vague resemblance between Balderston Hall and the Grand Central Terminal!"

"M'yes, but that is the cast, so to speak!"

"But, Bill," Liz said, "you're making it all sound as if the doctor were merely a passerby, and *I* thought that *he—did*n't he?"

"No." Leonidas decided that Fell's beady eyes weren't quite as viciously angry as they had been. "No, he didn't. If he had not first rushed out to Fenwick's kitchen with his Roquefort cheese, and then hunted around Fenwick's desk for 'Tamerlane'—but let us not lose sight of the fact that he thought of the cheese first. He does not, moreover, meet certain other specifications."

"With his hands all tied up," Mrs. Granby said, "how can you tell if he's right-handed or left-handed?"

"That," Leonidas told her, "is almost a side issue. Now what I really wish to know from you, Doctor Fell, is why you brought that cheese, which has been haunting me, and why you rushed away to return later, and if Fenwick mentioned during the course of your telephone conversation where he acquired his 'Tamerlane,' and finally, if you happened to see anyone else there on your first trip. Of course, I'd like to think that you could forgive our trespasses on your person—and not raise too much furor," he added. "Shaver, will you—er—stand by, just in case? Kilroy, remove his gag. My name, by the way, is Leonidas Witherall."

To the bewilderment of everyone in the room, Doctor Fell merely smiled pleasantly when his gag was taken off.

"I'll forgive you very willingly," he said. "I'm proud and happy to meet you, Mr. Witherall, and if my ankles weren't tied, I'd like to walk over and shake your hand, sir! You've given me a lot of happy hours."

The pince-nez fell from Leonidas's nose. He caught them absent-mindedly in mid-air.

"One of my life's ambitions," Fell went on, "has been to meet Morgatroyd Jones. Another of my life's ambitions has been to own a complete set of the works of Morgatroyd Jones. Firsts. And—"

"Hey!" Kilroy said suddenly. "Morgatroyd Jones! Hey, he writes Haseltine! They're the first books I ever read in the army! Hey—"

"Sssh!" Mrs. Mullet said reprovingly. "Sssh! Mr. Witherall writes them!"

"Oh, *le galant!*" Shaver said with a laugh. "*Le galant!* I should have guessed. The Brain! Only The Brain could have thought up *le galant!*"

"Firsts, *and* autographed," Fell continued.

"I do regret," Leonidas replaced the pince-nez, "that I have disposed of the only such set, doctor, but perhaps when this affair is over, you may be able to arrange some sort of dicker or trade with its current owner, a newcomer to your trade—"

"Who? What's his name?"

"Kilroy," Leonidas said. "Er—the large youth standing beside you."

"But, pal, I—"

"M'yes," Leonidas said, "Kilroy owns a complete set of Haseltine firsts, one hundred and seven of them, all autographed to the very hilt—don't be so modest about your achievement, Kilroy! I feel you made a very auspicious start when you acquired those books from me. Now, doctor, those odds and ends I wished to know about?"

"I came and found him and beat it, Mr. Witherall—and wouldn't you have, if you'd come to buy a 'Tamerlane,' and found the seller murdered? I hoped the cops would have come by the time I came again."

"Did he specifically say it was 'Tamerlane' which he had?"

"Yes—he was a little coy about it at first. People always are. They say it's 'worth coming to see.' As for that cheese—I just knew he liked it, and brought it as a present! We'd talked about cheeses the first time I met him, a couple of years ago in Boston. I came out and stayed overnight at Balderston Hall, and looked at his books— he's got some good ones. How'd you guess I was there before tonight?"

"You knew so much," Leonidas said, "about full iceboxes."

"Believe it or not, I went straight to the kitchen when I first came—" Fell paused. "I wonder if the boys would undo me now, so I could talk with you privately?"

A minute later, he carefully shut the door to Mrs. Granby's bedroom.

"Listen, Witherall," he said, "when I first went there.

I *did* go straight to the kitchen because the paper around that cheese had got torn, and the damn stuff was getting all over me! I stuck the thing into the icebox before I went into the library and saw Balderston lying there. Then you better believe I got that damn cheese and beat it, quick! My cab had gone, so I just walked around a thousand miles before I went back—so sure the cops would be there then! But listen, I *did* see someone when I first went into the kitchen—and of course, I couldn't tell the cops this without getting myself all involved!— and it was that fellow in there," he nodded toward the living room, "with the glasses. Shaver."

"And where was he?"

"I just saw his back as he went out the kitchen door," Fell said. "I thought it was Thor, at first. Then later I realized it couldn't have been. Thor was in the wine closet—and I'd forgotten he was so short. This fellow I saw was tall. I tell you, you've got the murderer right *in* there, Witherall!"

"I wonder," Leonidas said thoughtfully, "if your first visit did not precede Mrs. Granby's. M'yes. And I wonder if you have not perhaps made the same error which Fenwick made when he informed Thor that his *guest* was arriving—did it ever come out during any of the police questioning that Fenwick did not mention my name specifically, but said 'guest'?"

"A fat cop worked that out of Thor," Fell answered. "A sergeant. Seemed to be a great friend of yours—by the way, I'm sorry I used your name when I phoned the cops. But I was pretty well sunk at that point. I'd have used anyone's name!"

"Er—cancel your sorrow," Leonidas said, "in view of

223

the manner in which you have since been treated. M'yes, I think Fenwick was confused by a fleeting resemblance —and did he tell you how he acquired his 'Tamerlane'?"

"He told me it was a smart deal and he got it out of the teeth of another collector," Fell said. "Having had a few deals with Balderston myself, I'd say the literal translation was he'd gypped the hell out of some poor devil. Is the 'Tamerlane' really lost? I hate—"

He broke off as shouts arose from the living room.

"Bill!" Liz said as Leonidas rushed in. "Bill—Red wanted to show the dinosaur's footprint to her aunt after I explained what it was—and look! *Look!*"

She pointed to the brown paper wrappings, in which nestled— Leonidas hurriedly affixed his pince-nez.

"The bank report!"

"And a note to you attached with a paper clip!" Liz said.

"And in Fenwick's handwriting!" Mrs. Granby added.

Leonidas picked up the note.

" 'Dear Witherall,' " he read aloud, " 'I've asked young Shaver, the son of old friends of mine, to join us at dinner tonight. I wonder if you would look him over with some idea of seconding my proposal that he become a member of the Collectors' Club. His name might then be added, if you are willing, to the list of new candidates to be admitted tomorrow night at the meeting at your house. While he is not interested in books, I understand that he collects odd musical instruments and is a pianist of some ability. Since we have often deplored the lack of a decent accompanist in the club, we well might overlook his ignorance of books. Faithfully yours—'. M'yes. Now I wonder, Mrs. Granby, if you have a copy of today's *Dal-*

224

ton Chronicle? You do? And could you get it for me? I recall noting a list of prospective Collectors' Club members in it."

"But look here, it *was* a dinosaur's footprint!" Liz said. "When did it get to be a bank report? When was it a dinosaur's footprint *last?*"

"On my way from McLean's to the Dalton Inn. The murderer," Leonidas said, "merely switched packages on me—and is now in full, complete and undisputed possession of your dinosaur's footprint. Er—while it's an interesting change for him, and definitely an improvement over the bank report, it is still very far from being what he wanted. Now, since some of you have evinced a certain knowledge of the gallant Lieutenant Haseltine, perhaps you will recall that there is always a period when he thinks of Cannae—"

"Can I what?" June asked in some perplexity.

"C-a-n-n-a-e." Shaver spelled it out. "Cannae."

"Oh, *I* know all about Cannae," Liz said with pride. "It's something I missed entirely at Miss Clinch's, I might add. I picked it up from listening to Haseltine on the radio. Darling, if you'd only learn to listen to something but Benny Goodman and those awful swing bands, you'd learn so much! After the gallant lieutenant's been buffeted around by fate till he's practically a pulp, he thinks of Cannae and then he just solves everything!"

"What *are* you talking about, Liz?" June demanded. "What is Cannae, anyway? And what's it got to do with all of this?"

"Cannae," Leonidas said, "is the historic battle between the Romans and the Carthaginians, fought in Apulia in the year 216 B.C., in which the small, weak army of Hannibal cut the incomparable forces of eighty-five thousand proud Roman legionnaires to pieces—"

"To *shreds!*" Fell broke in. "Haseltine *al*ways says *shreds!*"

"M'yes, to shreds. In that," Leonidas continued, "by means of an ingenious strategical concentration, it caught the enemy from the flank with cavalry, and surrounded him. Clausewitz and Schlieffen of the Prussian General Staff elaborated the idea of Cannae into a general theoretical doctrine, then compressed the doctrine into an exact strategical system. Blitzkrieg, in short, without latter-day elaborations and decorations. Er—that is Cannae. That is the method which we will now attempt to use in getting him."

"Getting *who?*" Shaver demanded.

"Whom. Not who. Er—Harriman, of course. John Harriman. He killed Fenwick—ah, thank you, Mrs. Granby," he said politely as she gave him the Dalton newspaper. "The list of new members is on the back page. M'yes. Now let me see. Arlington, Beacon, Bolster, Gregory—m'yes, here he is! Harriman, John. Collector of books. M'yes. Quite!"

"Bill Shakespeare, you're crazy!" Shaver said. "Why, Harriman rescued you! He *rescued* you!"

"Twice. M'yes."

"Harriman!" June said. "Harriman—d'you mean that tall, good-looking boy who was in Mr. Balderston's office so long this morning? Why, it wasn't long after he left that Mr. Balderston brought me that package!"

"M'yes, I think we may take it for granted that Harriman is the one with whom Fenwick dealt so smartly. This evening, after learning to what extent he had been—

er—gypped, as Doctor Fell so aptly put it, he went to Balderston Hall. Fenwick, looking out the window, mistook him for Shaver arriving—and told Thor that he'd let in the guest who was coming. Not that Shaver and Harriman look at all alike, but because Fenwick was expecting a tall young man. I might add that I confused the two in the same casual manner. M'yes, Fenwick let Harriman in, unquestionably refused point-blank to make the slightest adjustment whatsoever in whatever arrangement he had made about 'Tamerlane'—whether he paid Harriman too small a price for it, or whether he merely —er—duped him, we can only guess. I—"

"But Fenwick would have been *right!*" Mrs. Granby interrupted. "He'd have been *right!*"

"I'm sure Fenwick would have been legally most correct," Leonidas agreed without hesitation. "Fenwick always was legally most correct. But Fenwick underestimated the human element, as he always did. And that—"

"And bingo," Kilroy said as he paused, "that was all, hey, pal?"

Leonidas nodded.

"Then consider," he said. "Consider. Just after returning home, Harriman looks out to see me, pursued, clutching what may for a moment have seemed to be a duplicate of his little brown paper package! And a posse, streaming at my heels. It is my feeling that at that point, he could not yet have had time to investigate the contents of his own package. But he was curious enough to rescue me and quiz me about mine. I informed him categorically that I had a bank report, and he took me to Fenwick's and let me out—why not? He was in no way involving himself by that gesture, and perhaps he welcomed the opportunity of having someone discover the situation which he'd left behind."

"What d'you suppose he did then?" Liz asked. "And d'you suppose he had an alibi?"

"I rather suspect," Leonidas said, "that he did this on the spur of the moment—and that things merely fell his way, like his entering Balderston Hall without being observed by Thor and Inga, and his luck in being able to shut them up in the wine closet without their seeing who he was. When he later discovered that he had the bank report, he was slated to do errands for his aunt, who was running that thing at the club. That at once hampered him, and helped him enormously."

"What on earth do you mean?" Liz asked.

"His presence at the club, and his busy, helpful rushing around there," Leonidas said, "was of great advantage to him. As Haseltine has so often remarked, a clever criminal does not take to the woods. He lets himself be seen by crowds, the while doing good constructive things. For crowds will so often agree with your estimate of where you were, and when you were there, and what you were doing. Neither Emily nor Yeoville nor anyone else at the club would ever believe that while Harriman was solving club problems, he also had ample opportunity to cruise around after me. Or that during his cruising, he spotted June, recognized her as Fenwick's secretary, and chased her in an effort to see if she could not provide some clew to the confusion of the little brown paper packages—don't ask me where he got the false beard, Liz, because I can't imagine! Possibly he just happened to have it with him, as Shaver had that violin!"

"But I can't get over it!" Liz said. "I mean, he saved you from the police! He *rescued* you!"

"M'yes, and how delighted he must have been when he picked me up outside the Inn," Leonidas said, "and found that I was still carrying my package!"

"But he brought you to the Country Club—"

"Never once meaning," Leonidas said, "to return and get me. It was his intention merely to leave me there—no doubt making some charming apology tomorrow for his getting stuck in a drift, or for his car breaking down. I was being side-tracked, just in case I might find out too much. M'yes, I can easily see where he got the Founder's Medal for Pleasing Personality and Unremitting Diligence. He's so charming that it took me some time to realize that he alone, of everyone I'd encountered, tried to dissuade me from attempting to solve this situation!"

"When did he switch the packages?" Shaver inquired.

"As I got out of his car at the club parking space, I rather think," Leonidas said. "In plain sight of Liz, although neither Harriman nor I guessed she was there. He asked me about my package with careful nonchalance— *why* was I still carrying it? And I, absorbed in the task of keeping my footing in these oversized overshoes, merely told him it was force of habit. I hadn't happened to tell him what was in it—we'd been very busy chatting about the storm, and the club. All data, now that I think of it, designed to uphold the aura of pleasant personality which he was displaying for my benefit. M'yes!"

"And then when he discovered that he had my dinosaur's footprint," Liz said, "he came back—and landed on June?"

"Exactly. If you'll consider," Leonidas said, "neither

Doctor Fell nor Mrs. Granby were in a position to know the club well enough to pick, as a hiding place for a victim, the laundry hamper of the service pantry of the dining room, with the latter's very convenient outside door! That required specialized knowledge of the place."

"How'd he get in? D'you suppose he had a key?" Liz asked.

"I dare say his aunt had the master key usually given anyone managing such an affair," Leonidas said, "and she probably gave it to him at some point. June, you and I were both very lucky. For Harriman and I had a brief discussion about murderers who jumped from the frying pan of one killing, so to speak, to the fire of another. He was deeply impressed by a quotation of mine from Haseltine, and I like to think that it may have convinced him of the futility of committing more murders. And now, for Cannae! We obviously must lure Harriman somewhere. Hm—not to my house. He'd be suspicious. And not too far away. And I must appear in some way connected—oh, I wish I knew if Harriman knows Emily and Yeoville!"

"They never mentioned knowing him, which is almost more important," Liz said. "They never listed him when they recited the names of all their Nice Neighbors for my benefit. And if they'd known him, I'm sure that they would have!"

"Haven't you any idea, Witherall," Fell said with a touch of plaintiveness, "where Balderston's 'Tamerlane' is? I keep brooding about it!"

"The old octopus of fate has permitted me to catch at many straws tonight," Leonidas said, "but he has not dropped any hints as to the location—"

He suddenly stopped short, and began to smile.

"If that expressive grin on your face means you think you know where that damned package is," June said, "I wish you'd tell me! After all, *I* was the person who lost it, and *I* haven't any idea where it went to!"

"The old octopus," Leonidas said, "has dropped hint after hint to me—m'yes, of course he has, the splendid creature! I intended to use the bank report as a lure for Harriman, but we may as well have the real thing. Now, this is going to call for some extremely careful planning— and we have just about enough time left of the sergeant's allotted two hours. M'yes. Now—"

"Look, Shakespeare," Shaver broke in, "*le galant* couldn't even cope with this on paper! You can't possibly—"

"Now, first," Leonidas went on briskly, "we must telephone the Pushings' house Liz, will you try them? If they answer, hang up, and I'll think of some other place. And if Mrs. Cranby could provide me with some Mercurochrome, or merthiolate, or possibly even some catsup— and a bit of her eye-shadow, too. Kilroy, you and Red and Mrs. Mullet and I will go in your car. Shaver, you take Liz and June and the doctor, and Mrs. Granby if she wishes to come. You do? M'yes. You'll proceed directly to Birch Hill Road and park in front of the Pushing establishment, Shaver. Liz will direct you. We will detour, and pick up 'Tamerlane' on the way."

"Just exactly what are you planning to do with the Pushings' French-Pseudish quarters?" Liz demanded. "No, I can't get them. The phone just rings and rings. Are you going to *use* their house? Oh, *really!* And suppose they come trooping home?"

"Shaver can be waiting to intercept them in the garage," Leonidas said. "I hardly like to ask Sergeant Mac-Cobble—illicit interception might so well threaten his pension. But we must remember to consult with him, too."

"I do not," Liz said, "understand *any* of this! Do you, Mrs. Mullet?"

"In my candied opinion," Mrs. Mullet said, "Mr. Witherall always knows what he's doing. I never knew him to fail with a Cannae *yet!*"

"I know that you, Liz, can imitate Emily's voice," Leonidas said. "You'll be Emily—don't interrupt, there isn't time! Doctor Fell will be Yeoville because of his mustache. M'yes, both of you bear a slight and fleeting physical resemblance to the originals. Fell must boom more—coach him on the way over, Liz. Mrs. Mullet will be their new maid—"

"They haven't any!" Liz said. "Theirs left today! Emily went into it in great detail. She hated their sherry and the Bendix grated on her nerves!"

"That household demands a maid," Leonidas said, "and I think Mrs. Mullet should have the fun of being it. She's missed so much—er—just sitting home here with Bappo. And the pistachio ice cream—yes, Liz, pistachio! June and Mrs. Granby and Red will be auxiliary troops —m'yes, they will have a little searching job to do, and also act as liaison with Sergeant MacCobble. Kilroy will stand by inside in case of violence. Now, Liz, when we get to Pushings', you will telephone—"

"Bill!" Liz said in honest horror. "Bill, you mean we're going to *break in?* But how can you?"

"With that galaxy of French doors," Leonidas said, "I've always asked myself wonderingly how any passerby could possibly refrain from it. Now, you are going to telephone Harriman at his aunt's house, and you are going to be Emily Pushing—"

"Suppose he's not home? What if he isn't there?"

Leonidas sighed.

"I wish I could make you understand that the octopus of fate wouldn't permit such a catastrophe after all his beneficence! He *intends* that this will succeed and that Meredith's shall have those fifty acres, don't you see? And if Harriman's not home, if we're destined for some slight set-back, we'll find him somehow, and lure him somehow, possibly utilizing Red's—er—assets. But I feel he will be home. In an agitated voice, you're to say you're Emily Pushing and speaking for Mr. Witherall, that I said Mr. Harriman knows what the situation is, and can he possibly come to your house, yes, Mrs. Pushing's, right away? You're so terribly upset, Mr. Witherall's calling for him, and please can he come—oh, Mr. Pushing says Mr. Witherall's fainted again—can he come, quickly! And hang up. Have you got it? Try it, please."

Liz's initial attempt was so highly successful that Kilroy looked anxiously at Leonidas, as if reassuring himself as to the state of his health.

"All Doctor Fell has to do is to boom, all Shaver has to do is to prevent Emily and Yeoville from getting into the house from the garage," Leonidas said. "I'll tell Red about the searching job on the way. Now, let us be off!"

Aʙᴏᴜᴛ ʜᴀʟғ ᴀɴ ʜᴏᴜʀ ʟᴀᴛᴇʀ, Harriman bounded up
Pushing's front walk and punched the doorbell with his
forefinger.

Mrs. Mullet was at the door in a flash.

"Are you the gintleman herself was calling?" she asked
nervously in the brogue she'd worked over from Carnavon to Dalton. "Oh, such a time it is we've been after
having, sor! The poor gintleman's in the parlor, this
way—"

Harriman seemed visibly moved at the sight of Leonidas, pallid, ashen, and gruesomely bloodstained, lying
on the living room sofa with Liz and Fell hovering wor-
riedly over him.

But Kilroy, poised behind a decorative screen and peering intently through a crack, noticed that Harriman's eyes
were focussed on the little brown paper-wrapped package on the table next the sofa.

"Good God, Shakespeare, what've you been doing to
yourself this trip? What's the matter?"

"Harriman," Leonidas moistened his lips, and with obvious effort raised himself to a sitting position, "Harriman, I've got to get away! I need your help!"

"What's happened, Shakespeare?" He was still looking
at the package.

"A policeman," Leonidas said. "He tried—tried to get
me. We struggled—his gun went off—I got away! Can

you get me to Boston? The house of friends of mine. I'll be safe for a while. I—I can walk—" He struggled bravely to his feet.

"Sure, I'll take you into Boston. Come along. Here—your package! Isn't this your package?"

"Don't touch that!" Leonidas said sharply. "Don't touch it—it's only that bank report! It's the omen of *all* my bad luck! It's the thing which began *all* my misfortunes—leave it alone! I never wish to see it again! Emily," he swayed slightly, "Emily, for my sake, for the peace of my mind, take that package and hurl it into your fireplace among the glowing embers! Burn it up now, before my eyes! I—"

As Liz started apparently to comply, Harriman snatched the package from her hand.

"No!" he said. "No! You don't burn that!"

"But Harriman!" Leonidas began. "I—"

"*I'm* taking this package, Shakespeare! And *you're* taking one on the button—"

His arms were suddenly pinned from behind.

"Yeah, pal?" Kilroy said. "You and who else, hey? Okay, Mr. Witherall. Relax. I got him. Where's that confession you wrote for him to sign? Got a pen? Okay, Harriman, the old John Hancock!"

Leonidas never quite knew where Kilroy was applying pressure, but Harriman seemed almost glad to sign his name with Doctor Fell's pen.

"Where's your cop?" Kilroy inquired. "Didn't Mrs. Mullet whistle for him yet, hey? Stop squirming, pal," he added to Harriman. "You'll only get hurt!"

"Here he is!" Leonidas said briskly as Sergeant Mac-Cobble marched in. "First on the scene, as usual! Here

235

you are, sergeant. The package is what he killed Fenwick Balderston for, and here is his signed confession. He will doubtless fill in the details for you—ah, Red, did you find the false beard out in his car?"

"Gee, yes," Red said, "and June and Mrs. Granby found the dinosaur's footprint, too! Gee, you look awful with that catsup and the eye-shadow! Did he fall for it all right?"

There was a little silence, broken by the click of the sergeant's handcuffs.

"He fell for it," Harriman said bitterly. "Any advices, Shakespeare, for the fly who walked straight into the parlor?"

"Pleasing personality and unremitting diligence," Leonidas told him, "are—er—not enough. Tell the truth, and fear no—"

"Is it all right to let them in now?" Shaver demanded from the doorway. "Because they resent me, and they resent all this, very much indeed!"

"Ha! What's the meaning of this, Witherall!" Yeoville pushed past Shaver. "What's—"

"To one," Leonidas said, "who adores the art of legerdemain, Yeoville, it should be a privilege to witness this scene, the finale of the Three Wonderful Packages Act. We'll tell you all tomorrow. We're really too tired now."

"See here!" Yeoville turned to Liz. "Mrs. Goldthwaite! Liz! What—"

Leonidas felt his head jerk up as if someone had landed an uppercut on his chin.

"Oh, Bill," Liz said, "I kept *mean*ing to tell you! George was Goldthwaite Steel Products, you know, and that's why I have to have that car, and the bodyguards. Dur-

ing the strikes, everyone is *so* unpleasant to the big stock-
holders—going around tipping my car over, and trying
to black my eyes, and all! And June and I are *both* cor-
porations—it's all George's fault—and we have to do
what those lawyers say. But I'm sure we can manage the
fifty acres! We've far too much land at Fairlawns, and
the lawyers will probably simply adore giving it to an
educational institution—so nice for taxes! Really, I meant
to tell you, and then—well, Smith—I mean, Kilroy—and
I thought it was rather *fun*—"

"Kilroy is one of those giants?" Leonidas demanded.
"Kilroy, why didn't you *say* something? You must have
recognized me!"

Kilroy shrugged. "I was off duty, pal, why should—"
He broke off as a clap of thunder shook the room.

"And lightning!" Yeoville rushed to the window, with
Emily running after him. "Look—chain lightning! Did
you ever see such a night? Snow, blizzard, thaw, slush—
and now thunder and lightning! I never saw anything like
it! I don't understand that thunder and lightning!"

"Er—I do," Leonidas said gently. "It's the old octopus
of fate, wrapping the—er—drapery of his couch about
him, and lying down to pleasant dreams!"

The next morning, Mrs. Mullet rapped sharply at the
study door.

"It's my candied opinion," she said as she entered,
"that you never went to bed at all, Mr. Witherall!"

"I didn't. There seemed," Leonidas said, "so little reason to!"

"I guessed you'd come right back and start the Haseltine! The Frigid News says Harriman's made a full and

complete confession—honest, Mr. Witherall, what a night! In one foul sweep, we got a murderer, and the land for Meredith's, and I *think* we got those two young couples going steady out of it, too. Is the story all straight in your mind now?"

"My original idea," Leonidas said, "was to take three packages, switch them, murder a Man of Distinction, and see what happened. Now I know. There's only the writing to do. The formula as before."

"And who does it any better?" Mrs. Mullet asked with spirit. "And what are you going to call it?"

"I dallied with 'The Dinosaur's Footprint,' and with 'Mammoth Stride'—a really bad pun," Leonidas said. "But I've decided on 'The Iron Clew.'"

"I don't get it!"

"That is in honor of the spot," Leonidas said, "where the paper boy who comes in the Cadillac put the little brown paper package—which he found on the ground where June lost it out of her car when she opened the door. Charles neatly—and mercifully—wrapped the evening paper around it, and thrust it into the outstretched iron hand of the iron hitching post boy at the gate of Balderston Hall. The major clew—and it literally stared everyone in the face all the time! And now, Mrs. Mullet, some coffee, please, while I start for the deadline of Opus One Hundred and Eight. M'yes, indeed. 'The Iron Clew'!"